# FAMILY TROUBLE . . .

Mr. Atwood shot Lisa a serious look as they turned and headed off through the crowded airport terminal. "And I know your mother is as concerned as I am about this whole college business."

Lisa bit back a groan. "I know that, too," she said carefully. "And I'd really like to tell you the reasons I made the choice I did. Then I'm sure you'll understand a little better. Maybe after we get home and have some lunch—"

"I think I understand your main reason well enough," her father replied with a slight frown. "I understand that your boyfriend is only a junior this year, and you don't want to go to school somewhere far away from him."

Lisa didn't answer. There was no need to, since her father was already going on about the importance of a good education in impressing future employers and business contacts.

*Maybe if I just let him go, he'll talk himself out in a few hours and we can get on with having a nice Thanksgiving.*

But she knew she was kidding herself. It was already painfully obvious that this visit wasn't going to be easy.

D1550957

**Don't miss any of the excitement
at PINE HOLLOW,
where friends come first:**

# PINE HOLLOW™

## CROSS-TIES

### BY BONNIE BRYANT

**BANTAM BOOKS**
NEW YORK • TORONTO • LONDON • SYDNEY • AUCKLAND

*Special thanks to Laura Roper of Sir "B" Farms*

RL: 5.0, AGES 12 AND UP

CROSS-TIES
*A Bantam Book / April 2000*

"Pine Hollow" is a trademark of Bonnie Bryant Hiller.

Text copyright © 2000 by Bonnie Bryant Hiller
Cover art copyright © 2000 by Alan Kaplan

All rights reserved. No part of this book may be reproduced or
transmitted in any form or by any means, electronic or mechanical,
including photocopying, recording, or by any information storage and
retrieval system, without permission in writing from the publisher.
For information address: Bantam Books.

If you purchased this book without a cover you should be aware that this
book is stolen property. It was reported as "unsold and destroyed" to the
publisher and neither the author nor the publisher has received any payment
for this "stripped book."

ISBN: 0-553-49301-9

**Visit us on the Web! www.randomhouse.com/teens**

**Educators and librarians, for a variety of teaching tools, visit us at
www.randomhouse.com/teachers**

*Published simultaneously in the United States and Canada*

Bantam Books is an imprint of Random House Children's Books, a division
of Random House, Inc. BANTAM BOOKS and the rooster colophon are
registered trademarks of Random House, Inc., Bantam Books, 1540
Broadway, New York, New York 10036.

PRINTED IN THE UNITED STATES OF AMERICA

OPM     10 9 8 7 6 5 4 3 2 1

*My special thanks to Catherine Hapka for her help in the writing of this book.*

# ONE

"Wait, Mom." Lisa Atwood glanced over her shoulder and spotted her mother struggling to lift a heavy garment bag out of the trunk. "Let me get that."

Lisa dropped her overstuffed carry-on suitcase on the sidewalk of the airport unloading zone and hurried toward the car. She grabbed the garment bag from her mother and, with some effort, managed to drag it over the lip of the trunk. Then, using both hands, she yanked it onto the sidewalk and leaned it against her carry-on bag.

"Thank you, dear," Mrs. Atwood said breathlessly. She reached into the trunk for the last bag, a small cosmetics case, and carried it over to the pile of luggage. "Now, wait here a moment while I take the car over to the short-term lot."

Dodging a family with several screaming toddlers and praying they weren't on her flight, Lisa slammed the trunk and joined her mother on the sidewalk. "I told you, Mom," she said as patiently

1

as she could manage. "You really don't have to wait with me. I'm seventeen, not seven, remember? It's not like I've never flown by myself before."

"Nonsense." Mrs. Atwood waved one hand briskly in the air, then headed toward the car. "Now, I won't be a moment."

Lisa sighed, knowing it was useless to argue. When her mother's mind was made up, there was usually no changing it. "All right," she called as Mrs. Atwood opened the driver's door. "But I'm going to get in line for my boarding pass. I'll meet you there, okay?"

Her mother gave another little wave, which Lisa took as assent. Glancing around as the car pulled away from the curb, Lisa soon spotted a line of metal carts that passengers could rent to transport their luggage inside. Looping the strap of her cosmetics bag over one arm and hoisting the carry-on over the other shoulder, she grabbed the handle of the garment bag and began to drag her unwieldy pile of luggage in the direction of the carts.

*Whew,* she thought, feeling beads of sweat spring to her forehead despite the cool November morning air. *Next time I let Mom help me pack, I'd better remember to borrow a horse or two from Pine Hollow to help me carry the load.* She smiled at the thought of asking Max Regnery, her longtime riding instructor and the owner of Pine Hollow Stables, to allow one of his finest riding horses—say,

Topside or Calypso—to come to the airport and act as Lisa's personal pack mule.

The strap of Lisa's carry-on bag was slipping down her arm. She shoved it back up onto her shoulder and took another few steps toward the row of carts, then lost her grip on her cosmetics case. She groaned and leaned over to pick it up.

"Need some help?" a male voice asked.

Lisa looked up to see a middle-aged man in a business suit gazing at her with concern. "Oh, no," she gasped politely. "I'm fine, thanks."

At that moment, the strap of her carry-on bag slipped off her shoulder again and the bag tumbled to the ground. Lisa lost her balance for a moment and loosened her grip on the cosmetics case, which also slipped out of her grasp and settled with a bounce at the man's feet.

He smiled sympathetically. "Don't kill yourself. Why don't you wait here while I fetch you a cart?"

"Um, thanks," Lisa said, her face red. "That would be great." Digging into the pocket of her jeans, she pulled out a handful of quarters. Her mother never let her go anywhere without enough emergency phone change to last a year.

The man accepted several quarters for the cart rental and strode off. He returned a moment later, pushing one of the carts. Despite Lisa's protests, he helped her pile her bags onto the cart.

"I could manage, really. I mean, I don't want to

3

make you late or anything," she said anxiously as he balanced her cosmetics bag in the top basket of the cart.

"No worries. I have plenty of time." The man glanced at her. "Besides, I have a daughter just about your age," he added. "What kind of father would I be if I ignored another young lady in distress?"

Lisa smiled. His words made her thoughts flash to her own father, far away in California. "Well, thank you very much," she told the man. "I really appreciate it."

"You're welcome." The man gave her a kind smile, his gray eyes twinkling. "Have a nice flight."

"You too." Lisa sent the man a little wave as he hurried off; then she grabbed the handle of the cart. After a quick glance up to make sure she was in the right area, she headed inside through the automatic glass doors. The airport was crowded, which Lisa supposed wasn't too surprising. It was the Saturday before Thanksgiving, and she was sure that many people, like her, had the week off from school or work and were traveling to be with their families.

*Or half their family, in my case,* she thought, shoving at the cart to push it over a bump in the floor. *Just one more super-thrilling thing about coming from a broken home—figuring out where to spend the holidays.*

She soon found the way to the line she needed and parked her luggage behind a group of girls just a couple of years older than she. They were dressed casually in jeans and sweatshirts, backpacks strapped onto their backs or duffel bags slung over their shoulders as they chatted eagerly. Lisa caught the words *midterms* and *roommate* as she zipped open her purse and fished out her tickets.

*College girls,* Lisa thought, the idea giving her a thrill and causing an anxious shudder at the same time.

She gulped as she remembered what lay ahead of her in California—a whole lot of discussion about her own college future. Just about everyone she knew had been shocked when she had decided to send her acceptance in early to Northern Virginia University, especially since she hadn't told anyone until after it was done. Her parents, especially, were convinced that she had been impulsive.

*Pretty ironic, really,* Lisa thought, shoving her cart forward a few feet as the line moved. *Trying to convince me I'm totally screwing up my life is just about the only thing Mom and Dad have been able to agree on since the divorce.*

Just as Lisa inched her way to the front of the line, her mother returned from parking the car. "Yoo-hoo!" she called cheerfully, weaving her way past people and luggage and waving her arms at Lisa like some kind of demented windmill.

Lisa winced, wondering if there was any way she could pretend not to see her mother. For the umpteenth time, she wished she'd tried a little harder to convince her mother that she could drive herself to the airport. But Mrs. Atwood had been cheerfully insistent on driving her. She claimed she only wanted to save Lisa the money she would have spent on long-term parking fees, but Lisa suspected that wasn't the whole story. Mrs. Atwood had taken her divorce pretty hard for a long time, and it didn't take a genius to figure out that she still wasn't comfortable having Lisa fly off to spend time with her father and his new family in California—especially for Thanksgiving.

"Whew!" Mrs. Atwood exclaimed loudly, fanning herself with her pocketbook as she joined Lisa in line. "It certainly is crowded here today. Why, you'd think there was a holiday coming up or something!"

She giggled at her own wit, glancing around to see if anyone else had heard her. Forcing herself to smile at the lame joke, Lisa pushed her cart forward as the college girls hurried toward the next available ticket agent. "It's almost my turn," she commented blandly.

"Hmmm." Mrs. Atwood checked her watch. "Well, don't worry, dear. You have plenty of time before they'll start boarding."

At that moment one of the people at the

counter gestured for Lisa to step forward. Before long she was checked in, boarding pass in hand and heavy garment bag on its way to the cargo hold.

"Okay," Lisa said, slinging her carry-on bag over her shoulder and glancing at her boarding pass. "I'd better head to my gate. You can take off if you want, Mom. I'm sure you've got better things to do today than hang around the airport."

Mrs. Atwood picked up Lisa's cosmetics case and followed her daughter away from the check-in counter. "Nonsense. I'll stay and keep you company until it's time to board. I have the whole day off today, and Rafe is working until six."

"Oh. Okay." Lisa cringed slightly at the mention of her mother's boyfriend. Rafe was a twenty-five-year-old college student who worked at the clothing store where Mrs. Atwood was an assistant manager, and he wasn't exactly one of Lisa's favorite people. She was glad that her mother was finally coming out of her depression over the divorce, but she wished she'd found somebody a little closer to her own age to help her do it.

As they walked through the busy airport toward Lisa's gate, Mrs. Atwood continued to chatter on about her plans with Rafe for that week. ". . . and then we both have to work on Black Friday, of course—that's the day after Thanksgiv-

7

ing," she explained cheerfully. "It's the busiest shopping day of the year, you know."

"Mmm." Lisa searched her mind for some way to change the subject. "Hey, Mom, speaking of shopping, what do you want for Christmas? They have some pretty cool stores out in L.A., and I—"

"Oh, whatever, dear." Mrs. Atwood waved one hand. "I always love the things you pick out for me, you know that." She giggled. "Now, Rafe, on the other hand . . . Did I tell you about the blouse he tried to talk me into buying last week? What a heart attack!"

"Yes, you told me about that," Lisa said, shifting her carry-on to her other shoulder and checking the number of the gate they were passing.

"Of course, his heart's in the right place, you know." Mrs. Atwood sighed happily and patted her hair. "He even offered to bring dessert on Thursday. Isn't that wonderful?"

"Sure." Lisa sighed, resigning herself to yet another long conversation about Rafe the Wonder Boy.

*Ugh,* she thought. *I really thought Mom would be tired of that long-haired goofball by now. But she just gets more and more into him every day. What's that about?*

She had no idea. As far as she could tell, Rafe's only real selling point was his appearance. She was sure that a lot of women would find his wavy dark hair and chocolate brown eyes appealing—at least until they actually spoke to him and discovered how lazy, self-satisfied, and generally vapid he really was.

*Still, I guess I should be grateful to Rafe,* Lisa reminded herself as she and her mother reached the right gate and found seats near the window overlooking the tarmac. Glancing outside, she saw that her plane was just taxiing toward the gate. *If Mom didn't have him to hang out with this week, she'd probably spend the whole time brooding over how I'm off in sunny California with the guy who ruined her life. Or better yet, figuring out new and improved ways to tell me that I'm ruining my life by going to NVU next year.*

She considered it something of a miracle that her mother's snippy comments about her choice of school had tapered off in the past few days. Then again, maybe she was kidding herself.

*She probably just figures Dad will take care of it,* Lisa thought. *That's how she dealt with a lot of the really sticky stuff when they were married. And maybe not much has changed, at least when it comes to problems concerning me.*

As if reading her mind, Mrs. Atwood suddenly interrupted her own description of Rafe's new college seminar and turned to gaze at Lisa seriously. "By the way, Lisa, I don't want you to think that just because Rafe is so happy at NVU, I think it's the right school for you. I do hope your father can make you understand how serious this college business is." Mrs. Atwood frowned slightly. "If there's one thing he's good at, after all, it's reminding one of the harsh realities."

Gritting her teeth, Lisa forced herself to let the comment pass. Soon she would be boarding her flight, and then she wouldn't have to listen to her mother's comments about her college choice—or Rafe—for a whole week. Of course, after a couple of days of listening to her father's comments, she might be longing for tales of good old Rafe. . . .

*I suppose I should look on the bright side,* she thought. *It's not as if anyone else is off on some great, wonderful, perfect Thanksgiving vacation this year.*

She shook her head sympathetically as she remembered that her two best friends and her boyfriend were all grounded. Stevie Lake and her twin brother, Alex, who was also Lisa's boyfriend of ten months, had thrown a party when their parents weren't home. There had been drinking at the party, and, needless to say, Mr. and Mrs. Lake hadn't been pleased when they got a call from the police after neighbors complained about the noise. They also weren't pleased when they arrived home and discovered that the partyers had made a shambles of their house. That had all happened a month earlier, and Stevie and Alex were still grounded, with no idea when they would be free again. The punishment hadn't been easy on Lisa and Alex's relationship, especially since they'd been having a few problems before that.

Carole Hanson hadn't had anything to drink at the party, which wasn't too surprising. Lisa had always thought that her friend was eminently sensible and also possessed a sweet, almost childlike quality that sometimes made her seem much younger than her seventeen years. However, Carole had managed to get herself into deep trouble in another way. She had cheated on a test at school. Lisa sort of understood why Carole had done it—if her grade had slipped, she would have lost her riding privileges—but she still couldn't quite believe that honest, earnest Carole could actually stoop to cheating. Colonel Hanson, Carole's widowed father, had been equally shocked and had grounded Carole until New Year's, even banning her from the stable.

*Oh, well,* Lisa thought, feeling a bit depressed at the image of all her friends moping around at home during their Thanksgiving break. *Maybe at least Scott and Callie will have a nice time on their trip. Too bad they're not going to the same part of the West Coast as I am. I have a feeling I'll be needing some moral support before the week is out.*

She was a little surprised to catch herself having that thought. When Scott and Callie Forester had moved to Willow Creek, Virginia, the summer be-

11

fore, Lisa and Callie hadn't hit it off that well. Callie's older brother, Scott, was easier to warm up to. Like his congressman father, Scott had a real knack for connecting with people, and Lisa had felt comfortable with him right away. But these days, she thought of Callie as a real friend, too.

At her elbow, she sensed her mother fidgeting. A second later, Mrs. Atwood put a hand on Lisa's arm. "Will you be all right for a moment, dear?" she asked. "I'm going off in search of some coffee. Rafe and I were out pretty late last night."

Lisa willed herself not to cringe at that. Instead, she smiled calmly. "Sure, Mom. I'll be fine."

"Can I bring you anything?" Mrs. Atwood said, standing. "The food on your flight will probably be terrible."

"It's okay," Lisa replied. "I'm not very hungry."

As her mother hurried off in the direction of the nearest snack bar, Lisa returned her gaze to the window and her thoughts to her friends. Because of the grounding, she'd barely had a chance to say good-bye to Alex before leaving. The afternoon before, they'd managed to meet on the way home from their respective schools—Alex, like Stevie, Callie, and Scott, attended a private school called Fenton Hall—and spend a few moments together. But the all-too-brief meeting had been a little tense and awkward. Lisa could sense that Alex was unhappy about her going to California, as he always was, because it meant they would be apart. And then, of course, there was Skye. . . .

*I told him Skye wasn't going to be around this visit,* she thought, staring at a small plane taxiing past outside.

But she wasn't really seeing the plane. She was seeing Skye Ransom's handsome face that sunny California afternoon the previous summer when the actor had hinted that he wished they could be more than friends.

Even thinking about that conversation made her feel a little disloyal to Alex. *That's ridiculous,* she thought, irritated. *I made it clear to Skye then that it wasn't going to happen. And he was fine with that. I mean, he's been my friend for years. I've told Alex that over and over.*

She sighed, her anger passing as quickly as it had come. She wasn't even sure whom she was annoyed with, anyway—Alex for being jealous of her friendship with the handsome actor, or herself for letting his jealousy get to her.

She decided it didn't matter one way or the other. She'd spoken to Skye on the phone a couple of days earlier and discovered that he was just on his way out of town on a publicity jaunt for his television show, *Paradise Ranch.* He would be touring towns and cities all over the United States right through the Thanksgiving holiday. Lisa was disappointed that she wouldn't get to see him, but she guessed it was just as well. It would be nice not to have to deal with that particular issue when she returned home to Alex.

Mrs. Atwood came back with her coffee just as the gate attendants announced that Lisa's plane was ready to begin boarding. "Oh, my," Mrs. Atwood said, looking flustered. "But we didn't even get a chance to talk."

"We'll talk when I get back, Mom," Lisa said. To herself she added, *Probably about how dreamy Rafe is, as usual. And how handsome he looked carving the turkey. Major ick!*

"All right, sweetie." Mrs. Atwood set down her coffee and wrapped Lisa in a tight hug, then bent to gather up her things. "Here, I'll help you carry."

"It's okay, I've got it," Lisa insisted, trying to grab her cosmetics case from her mother's grasp. She was relieved when she turned the corner of the boarding gate and headed for the plane's door.

*At least Mom can't follow me any farther,* she thought, glancing over her shoulder as if to make sure her mother wasn't hurrying up the ramp after her.

Soon she was making her way down the narrow aisle of the plane, looking for row twenty-seven. The plane was crowded, but when Lisa found her row, she discovered she was the first to arrive. She pulled a magazine out of her carry-on, then stowed the bag in the overhead compartment and took her place by the window.

"Well, hello there!" a cheerful voice said.

Lisa glanced up and saw the friendly business-man who'd helped her earlier with the cart. She smiled at him. "Hi! Looks like we're on the same flight."

"Looks like we're in the same row," the man corrected with a smile. He gestured at the middle seat in Lisa's row. "This is me."

The man sat down and introduced himself as Roger Martin, explaining that he was only travel-ing as far as Dallas, the plane's stopover. "I'm go-ing to a family reunion," he explained. "My wife and kids got there a few days ago, but I had a meeting at work that I just couldn't miss."

Lisa introduced herself and said, "I'm going to visit my father for Thanksgiving. He lives in Cali-fornia. Where's your family reunion?"

The man smiled. "Well, that's the interesting part," he said. "It's at some kind of dude ranch down there in Texas. I've never been on a horse in my life! I'm a little nervous, especially since the whole family will be there with cameras."

Lisa laughed. "Don't worry," she assured him. "I ride a lot, and it's really not as hard as it looks, especially at a dude ranch. The horses there are used to beginners."

"Well, that's good to know," Mr. Martin said,

looking a little relieved. "The way my daughter has been talking, I was afraid they'd stick me on some kind of wild bucking bronco." He settled back in his seat as the flight attendants made their way up and down the aisle, checking that everyone's seat belt was secure before takeoff. "So, you said you're a rider," he added to Lisa. "Do you have your own horse?"

Lisa hesitated. That question brought up a lot of painful recent memories. The horse she'd always wanted to own, a beautiful Thoroughbred named Prancer, had died from complications of pregnancy just a week earlier. The memory of Prancer's willing spirit and gentle, loving soul brought tears to Lisa's eyes, as it always did these days, but she blinked them back before her seatmate could notice. "No," she answered carefully. "Um, I ride the school horses at the stable where I take lessons. There are some really great ones there."

"That's nice," Mr. Martin said cheerfully, obviously unaware of Lisa's flash of sadness. The plane was taxiing down the runway, and he leaned forward to peer out the small window before returning his attention to Lisa. "So do you have any favorites?"

Lisa nodded, willing away an image of Prancer. "Sure," she said. "There's Barq, and good old Chip. And I really like Eve—she's this sweet gray mare. Also, a couple of my friends have their own horses, and I've ridden them a few times. Their names are Starlight and Belle."

The man looked a little confused. "Did you say one of the horses' names is Bark?" he said. "As in, arf arf, good pup?"

Lisa laughed. "It's *B-A-R-Q*," she explained. "*Barq*. It's the Arabian word for lightning. Barq is an Arabian horse with a lightning-shaped blaze."

"Ah!" The man smiled. "Okay, now that makes a little more sense. So how long have you been riding, Lisa?"

"Since I was thirteen." Lisa realized she was actually starting to feel calmer and more relaxed than she'd been in days. *I know exactly what Carole would say about that,* she thought with a secret smile. *She'd say that talking about horses makes any day better. And I guess maybe she's right.*

"Michael, are you totally deaf?" Stevie Lake asked irritably, glancing into the living room from the hallway. "If that TV was any louder, those stupid cartoons of yours would be breaking the sound barrier." She took another swipe at the hall's hardwood floor with a paper towel, rubbing in the last few spots of cleaner.

"I have to have it loud," Stevie's thirteen-year-old brother replied without glancing away from the TV screen. He was sitting on the living room couch with his feet propped up on the family's golden retriever, Bear, who was sound asleep on the rug. "I figure you and Alex will be breaking out the vacuum cleaner any second now."

Stevie's twin brother, Alex, walked down the hall toward her just in time to hear Michael's comment. He rolled his eyes. "Good guess, twerp," he muttered. He glanced at Stevie. "When I went to the kitchen to rinse out the bucket, Mom said we should meet her in there." He jerked his head in the direction of the living room. "She wants to talk to us. Probably about, like, how we missed a spot when we scrubbed out the fireplace."

"Ugh." Stevie sighed and wadded up her paper towel, rocking back on her heels and rubbing her neck. She glanced at her watch. "I can't believe this. It's eight-fifteen in the morning and I'm already exhausted."

"Right." Alex looked just as disgruntled as Stevie felt. "But don't forget, that's eight-fifteen on a *Saturday* morning."

"Eight-fifteen on a Saturday morning at the start of a holiday week," Stevie corrected. "Everybody we know is celebrating having a week's break from school, and what are we doing?"

Alex shrugged. "The same thing we've been doing for the past million years," he mumbled.

Stevie's fist tightened around the soggy paper towel. "It just doesn't seem fair, does it?" she said. "I mean, okay, I know we made a major mistake with that party. But still, do we really have to pay with all of our holidays? First Halloween, now Thanksgiving—how many holidays are we going to spend working our fingers to the bone when we should be out having fun?"

Alex shrugged again and glanced over his shoulder. "I think I hear Mom coming," he said. "Come on, let's see what thrilling stuff she has lined up for us this weekend."

He led the way into the living room. After tossing her paper towel into the garbage bag, Stevie followed and flopped onto the couch beside Michael.

"Hey! Watch it!" Michael shot her an irritated glance, and even Bear lifted his head for a moment and blinked at her. "I'm trying to watch TV here, you know," Michael snapped. "And aren't you two supposed to be working?"

"Not right now," Mrs. Lake said, striding in. "I need to talk to your brother and sister about something." She went to the TV set and switched it off.

"Hey!" Michael complained. But at a stern glance from his mother, he just sighed loudly and slunk out of the room, followed by the dog.

"Thanks, Mom," Stevie said. "You may have just saved that boy's hearing."

"Hmmm." Mrs. Lake glanced at the doorway. "Yes, well. Your father should be along soon. He wanted to be here for this."

"Be here for what?" Alex asked, folding his arms and leaning back against the edge of the bookcase.

Mrs. Lake didn't answer. Instead, she walked to the doorway and looked out into the hall.

Stevie gave her mother a curious glance, wondering what was going on. Had she discovered some chore for them that was so awful she needed backup to tell them? Or were she and Mr. Lake planning to rent Stevie and Alex out to the neighbors as a kind of roving teenage cleaning squad?

Suddenly another possibility occurred to Stevie. *Yikes,* she thought nervously. *I hope she didn't hear somehow about that time back in August when I sneaked out to meet Phil when I was supposed to be spending the night at Carole's. If she did, she's probably going to tell us that we're grounded for the rest of our natural lives. Or at least that I am.*

Taking another peek at her mother, though, Stevie felt a little better. Mrs. Lake didn't look angry or upset. In fact, she looked downright relaxed. Instead of one of the tailored suits she wore during the week to her law office, she was dressed casually in corduroys and a lightweight sweater. Her dark blond hair, still the same shade as Stevie's own, was pulled back in a couple of barrettes, giving her a youthful look.

Finally Stevie couldn't hold back her curiosity any longer. "So what's this all about, anyway?" she said. "Can't you at least give us a hint?"

"A hint," Mrs. Lake repeated thoughtfully. "A hint? No, I don't think so."

Stevie shot Alex a worried look. Their mother was usually plainspoken: It wasn't like her to be so vague. In fact, she was acting downright weird. What was going on?

Before she could come up with any new theories, Mr. Lake walked in. He glanced at his wife. "Did you tell them yet?"

Mrs. Lake shook her head. "I thought we should both be here for this."

"Good." Mr. Lake looked pleased. He clasped his hands behind his back and gazed at the twins. "Well then."

Stevie thought that if her parents didn't hurry up and spill whatever it was they wanted to say, she was going to scream. "Okay, here we are," she said. "So what is it? Do we have to disinfect the septic tank or something?"

"Don't give them any ideas," Alex muttered.

Mr. and Mrs. Lake laughed. "No, nothing like that," Mrs. Lake said.

"In fact, it's good news." Mr. Lake cleared his throat. "You see, your mother and I have been discussing your sentence, and we both think you two have really been quite mature about taking responsibility for your actions and serving your time accordingly."

"Most of the time, anyway," Mrs. Lake added

21

with a slight smile. "But complaints or no, you've been pretty good."

Mr. Lake grinned. "Right. Besides, our whole house is spotless, thanks to all those extra chores of yours. So we've decided to give you an early parole for good behavior."

Stevie gasped. "Are you serious? We're free?"

"We're not grounded anymore?" Alex asked at almost the same time.

Mr. and Mrs. Lake laughed. "You got it," Mrs. Lake said. "You're both free. Just remember, the next time you do anything like that . . ."

"Don't worry, Mom," Stevie said. "There won't be a next time. We've learned our lesson!"

"Totally," Alex agreed. He jumped to his feet. "So does this mean we can leave, like, now? Use the phone, whatever?"

"Sure does," his father assured him. "So what are you waiting for?"

"Just this," Stevie said, hopping over the coffee table and grabbing her parents for a group hug. "Thanks, guys!" Then she loosened her grip and raised her arms in the air. "Yippee! We're free!"

# TWO

Carole Hanson smothered a yawn as she climbed out of her car in the parking lot of a local shopping center. It was amazing to her that she could feel so tired after a full night's sleep. Any other Saturday morning she would have been at the stable for hours already. But somehow, doing anything else at eight-thirty on a Saturday morning seemed a lot less reasonable compared to staying in bed.

*It's hard to believe that exactly one week ago today I was on my way to the Colesford Horse Show,* she thought, reaching around to check on her thick black braid. She'd been so sleepy while plaiting it that she wasn't sure she'd remembered to snap a rubber band around the end. *It seems more like a year ago. Or maybe a decade.*

"Carole! Over here!"

Carole turned and saw the vice principal of her school, Dr. Durbin, waving at her from beside a large white van. Several other adults were clustered around the vehicle, many of them holding steaming plastic cups of coffee.

Giving Dr. Durbin a quick wave in response, Carole locked her car door and headed toward the group. She vaguely recognized most of the people around the van from the Hometown Hope meeting she'd attended earlier in the week. Carole had joined the volunteer group at her vice principal's suggestion as a way to avoid further punishment for cheating on a history test. That was why she was standing in a chilly parking lot that morning, preparing to head across town with the group to clean up a run-down park.

*Now all I have to do is survive the day somehow without going crazy,* she thought glumly. *And then start working on surviving tomorrow, and the next day, and the one after that, and the one after that. . . .*

She sighed, trying to block out the image of the days reeling forward, far into the future. Empty days. Days without the joy and comfort of everything she cared about most—horses, friends, fun. Maybe this Hometown Hope project would at least distract her enough so that she wouldn't spend every single second of the day longing for everything she'd lost.

"Good morning, Carole," Dr. Durbin said when Carole reached the adults. "Glad to see you here bright and early."

"Glad to be here," Carole lied, forcing a smile. She definitely wanted to stay on Dr. Durbin's good side. The vice principal was known to be tough and Carole was sure it was only her own otherwise spotless record that had allowed her a relatively painless punishment.

*After all, it could be worse,* she reminded herself, smiling politely as Dr. Durbin introduced her to the other adults standing with her. *I could be sitting in weekend detention right now. Or I could be suspended—Dad would just love that. He'd probably tack another month onto my grounding.*

If those thoughts were supposed to make her feel better about being where she was, they didn't work. Carole wasn't sure anything would make her feel better just at the moment.

*Well, except maybe wrapping my arms around Starlight and giving him a hug,* she thought glumly. *And we all know that's not going to happen anytime soon.*

Suddenly realizing that everyone was staring at her, Carole snapped back to the here and now. "Huh?" she blurted out.

Dr. Durbin gave her a careful look. "Mr. Jackson just asked if this is your first volunteer experience," the vice principal said.

"Oh! S-Sorry," Carole stammered. "Er, I guess I'm still a little sleepy." She had no idea which of the several men standing around was Mr. Jackson, so she smiled vaguely at all of them. "And yes, this is my first time. I mean, I've helped with some horseback-riding-type stuff, like Free Rein—you know, the therapeutic riding center. Oh, and I've done a few things for the local animal rescue place. But nothing like Hometown Hope."

"I've done some work for the County Animal Rescue League, too," commented an older woman with bright blue eyes. "If you enjoyed that, sugar, I'm sure you'll love this, too."

"Mmm-hmm," Carole said noncommittally. She wasn't expecting to love anything about the next few weeks. As she saw it, the most she could hope for was surviving them somehow without going nuts.

As the adults chatted about past Hometown Hope projects, another van pulled into the parking lot with a young man at the wheel. "Well now. There's Craig," Dr. Durbin said, glancing over at the newcomer. "Guess that means it's time to get this show on the road."

Carole barely glanced at Craig Skippack, the leader of the group, as he climbed out of the driver's seat. She was busy thinking about her own bad luck. Yes, it was better to be out in the fresh air, getting some exercise, doing some good, than to be sitting at home or in detention. But why couldn't Dr. Durbin be involved with something like Free Rein instead of Hometown Hope? Then at least Carole would get to be around horses.

*Yeah, right,* she thought. *Fat chance that Dad would have agreed to letting me volunteer at another stable, no matter how good the cause.* She knew that her father blamed her involvement with Pine Hollow for her problem at school. *And is he wrong about that?* she asked herself. *I mean, if I hadn't been so worried about not being able to ride . . .*

She shook her head, as if by doing so she could shake the whole topic out of her mind. She'd been over and over her transgression a million times. What good did it do to worry about why she'd cheated? She'd done it, and now she was paying for a moment's bad judgment with a month of misery. That was all she needed to know.

The whole group gathered around, and Craig gave a little speech about the project they were starting. Carole zoned in and out during the whole thing, trying to blend in at the back of the group and look as if she were paying attention.

Finally the group leader stopped talking and asked if there were any questions. When nobody had any, Craig shrugged and ran one hand over his thinning hair. "Okay, then, great," he said cheerfully. "Let's pile in and get going!"

The other volunteers let out a ragged but enthusiastic cheer, and Carole forced a smile onto her face. She didn't want anyone to notice how miserable she was. Nobody would understand. It was a Saturday morning, and she should be riding.

The entire group somehow crammed itself into the two vans. Carole found herself perched on the edge of the rear seat of Craig's van, squeezed between the metal wall of the vehicle and a thin young man with wire-rimmed glasses and wavy brown hair.

"Wow," the young man said jokingly. "I think we should call this thing the Sardine Can Van."

Carole nodded and smiled politely, then turned to look out the tiny porthole window nearby, hoping to end any potential conversation before it could begin. She knew the young man was just being friendly, and she felt a little guilty about acting so rude. But she just couldn't work up the energy to trade friendly conversation with anyone or force a laugh at anyone's lame jokes. She was focusing all her energy on not bursting into tears at the thought of being there, of being stuck picking up trash and painting rusty old playground equipment, rather than doing what she had loved doing almost every other Saturday morning for the past eleven years or so.

*The younger kids are probably starting their Pony Club meeting right about now,* she thought. *It's a mounted meeting this week, which means Rachel will be on Starlight.*

She sighed, picturing her spunky bay gelding

trotting around Pine Hollow's schooling ring with Rachel Hart in the saddle. She knew she should be spending every spare moment thanking her lucky stars that she'd found such a good solution to her problem. After all, Rachel was a good rider and probably the most responsible junior-high-age rider at Pine Hollow. It was lucky that she was trying to convince her parents to buy her a horse and was eager to prove how responsible she could be in caring for one. That had made her quick to accept Carole's proposal—free riding on Starlight during Carole's grounding in exchange for basic care and attention.

But knowing all that didn't make it any easier for Carole to accept that it would be almost six weeks before she would be allowed to ride her own horse—or even see him. It didn't make her feel much better about being banned from the place that had become as much of a home to her as her own house.

As she stared blankly out the window, tuning out the lively conversation around her, Carole suddenly noticed that they were turning down Quarry Road. Her heartbeat quickened slightly as she realized that they would be passing right by the turn-off onto Township Line Road. From there, it was less than a quarter mile to the gates of Pine Hollow.

Craning her neck, she peered out as the van

made the turn and approached the intersection. But it was no good. The road curved gently just beyond the turn, denying Carole even the quickest glimpse of the stable's land. All she could see as the van rumbled past Township Line Road was a couple of houses, a small field with the stubbly remains of the previous summer's corn crop, and a thick grove of evergreens beyond.

She sat back as far as her cramped position allowed, letting out a weary sigh. She didn't feel like looking out the window anymore. Closing her eyes, she thought about the park they were going to fix up. It was a couple of blocks beyond Whitby Street, the unofficial dividing line between the main section of Willow Creek and the one most people tried to pretend didn't exist—an area of run-down homes and decrepit trailers where most of Carole's friends had rarely, if ever, been.

But Carole had ventured across Whitby not too long before, when she had followed Ben Marlow there from Pine Hollow. Ben was the stable's youngest full-time stable hand—just a couple of years older than Carole. He kept to himself, and most people were happy to let him. But Carole had sensed a kindred spirit in the taciturn stable hand after seeing the incredible love and respect he had for horses, and horses for him. That was why she couldn't seem to resist trying to befriend Ben, even though he didn't make it very easy. One day, curious about his life outside the stable, she'd followed him home and discovered that he lived with an older man—his grandfather, perhaps?—in a tiny, battered house. A house just a block or two from the same park where she was headed now.

Carole's stomach lurched at the thought that she might run into Ben sometime this week. What would she do? What would *he* do? A week ago, the answer wouldn't have seemed too important. But a week ago, Ben hadn't kissed her and then looked through her as if she didn't exist. A week ago, Carole might not have known exactly where she stood with him, but she would have felt confident in saying they were friends of some sort. Now she wasn't even sure they were that.

Still, there wasn't much she could do about it one way or another. *If I see him, I'll just have to deal with it,* she thought. *Who knows? Maybe I'll even be able to figure out what's going on.*

There wasn't any more time to think about it. They were turning down Whitby Street, and a moment later Craig parked at the curb at the edge of the park, the van's tires crunching over a discarded aluminum can as he brought the vehicle to a stop.

Carole climbed out of the van with the others and looked around. The park, which was empty— it was early on a chilly morning—took up a full town block. It consisted of a wide open space with a few scraggly trees here and there. Some ancient

31

playground equipment was clustered in the middle, where several paths converged. Once upon a time, the playground and the paths had been paved with blacktop, but now weeds poked through so thickly that the hard, cracked surface was all but hidden from view. Most of the rest of the park looked as though it might have been a lawn at some point, but the grass had long since given up trying to grow, and all that remained was hard-packed dirt. As Carole and the rest of the Hometown Hope crew wandered across the sidewalk, a slight breeze rustled the abandoned newspapers scattered here and there and sent candy wrappers and other small debris scuttling across the dirt and into the street.

"Wow," Carole commented, forgetting her problems for a moment at the sight. "This place really is a mess."

A volunteer standing nearby heard her and nodded. She was a moon-faced young woman with wheat-colored hair gathered in a thick ponytail at the nape of her neck. "Isn't it awful?" she said in a soft, musical voice. "Imagine the poor children who have nowhere else to play. Doesn't it break your heart?"

Carole nodded, but the woman didn't really seem to expect a response. In fact, she was already pulling a pair of heavy work gloves out of her jeans pocket and hurrying toward Craig, who was handing out brooms, rakes, and trash bags.

Heaving a sigh and taking one more look around the depressing park, Carole headed that way herself. Craig had asked everyone to bring work gloves, but Carole had forgotten until that morning just before she left. Her father was sleeping in and she didn't want to wake him to ask where his work gloves were, so she had decided that her oldest pair of winter riding gloves would have to do. Now, grabbing them out of her back jeans pocket, she pulled them on and then accepted the rake Craig handed her.

"Why don't you join the group over at the playground, Carole?" he suggested. "Looks like there's a lot of garbage piled up around the merry-go-round. And you'll want to collect the fallen leaves, too—it'll make it much easier to paint and stuff."

"Sure," Carole said, heading toward the playground. Several other volunteers were there already, sweeping and raking, and Carole threw herself into the work of helping them.

After a while, a flash of movement caught her eye. Glancing over, she saw a clutch of children standing on the sidewalk just outside the park, curiously watching the volunteers. There were half a dozen or so all together, all shapes and sizes. Carole's gaze was drawn to the smallest child in the group, a tiny girl with impossibly large, dark eyes and a cloud of messy dark ringlets.

Carole couldn't help smiling. The girl gazed at her shyly for a moment, then returned the smile briefly before ducking behind a bigger girl to hide.

*Poor thing,* Carole thought. *If this is her idea of a good place to play, I'm really glad we're trying to make it a little better.*

The thought didn't stay with her for long, though. She had other things to think about. Like how she was going to survive more than a month away from the stable.

*Actually, it's five weeks, three days, and, oh, about fifteen hours,* she thought glumly as she attacked another pile of trash, trying to get as much benefit as she could out of the physical exercise. *But who's counting?*

Lisa took a deep breath and clutched the handle of her carry-on tightly as she walked down the jetway toward the terminal. Mr. Martin had disembarked in Dallas as planned, and nobody had boarded to take his seat. The elderly woman in the aisle seat had been sound asleep within moments of takeoff. Lisa had tried to read her magazine after that, but she hadn't been able to concentrate on anything except the coming reunion with her father. On the one hand, she couldn't wait to see him—it had been a long three months since her last visit with him and her baby half sister, Lily.

On the other hand, this wasn't going to be just another visit. Lisa was feeling more and more apprehensive about the inevitable college lectures. Was she really ready to hear, all over again, how foolish her decision was to commit to NVU so early?

After a moment's hesitation, Lisa stepped off the ramp and into the terminal. "Lisa!" a familiar voice called almost at once.

"Dad!" For a second, as she turned and spotted her father hurrying toward her, Lisa allowed herself to feel all the joy and relief she always felt at seeing him these days. She dropped her bag and grabbed him in a hug.

He hugged her tightly for a long moment, then stepped back and picked up her carry-on. "It's great to see you, honey," he said. "How was your flight?"

"Fine."

"Good. Now, can I assume you have several dozen suitcases to pick up at baggage claim?"

"You got it. You know Mom," Lisa replied lightly.

"Yes, I do." Mr. Atwood shot her a serious look as they turned and headed off through the crowded terminal. "And I know she's as concerned as I am about this whole college business."

35

Lisa bit back a groan. Couldn't he even wait until they got to the car? "I know that, too," she said carefully. "And I'd really like to tell you the reasons I made the choice I did. Then I'm sure you'll understand a little better. Maybe after we get home and have some lunch—"

"I think I already understand your main reason well enough," her father replied with a slight frown. "I understand that your boyfriend is only a junior this year, and you don't want to go to school somewhere far away from him."

"Dad!" Lisa winced. "You know me better than that. Yes, it will be nice to be close to Alex—and a lot of other people, too, like Mom and my other friends. But that was only a small part of the reason I chose NVU. There are a lot of wonderful things about that school, you know, if you just stop and think about it for a second."

"There are plenty of terrific things about *all* the schools on your list," Mr. Atwood countered, glancing at her as they walked. "And the plain fact is, most of them are a whole lot better overall, academically speaking, than NVU, no matter what other things it has going for it. Wouldn't you agree?"

Lisa didn't answer. There was no need to, since her father was already going on about the importance of a good education in impressing future employers and business contacts.

*Maybe if I just let him go on, he'll talk himself out in a few hours and we can get on with having a nice Thanksgiving,* she thought as they finally reached the baggage claim area and her father interrupted his lecture to hurry ahead and check for Lisa's luggage. *Maybe he just needs to get it out and then he'll listen to me for a change. And then he'll let it go.*

But she knew she was kidding herself. It was already painfully obvious that this visit wasn't going to be easy.

# THREE

"Ugh." Alex wrinkled his nose as he hoisted a pitchfork full of soiled straw and heaved it at the wheelbarrow just outside the stall in which he was standing. "You know, I'm starting to think that being ungrounded feels an awful lot like being grounded. Work, work, and more disgusting and smelly work."

Stevie shot him a disgruntled look. "Stop complaining," she said. "You're the one who practically begged to come to Pine Hollow with me. I can't help it if Max likes everyone to pitch in and make themselves useful instead of just standing around. I also can't help it if Belle decided she didn't feel like holding it in just for your benefit."

She patted her horse, a spirited bay mare who was currently cross-tied in the aisle outside her stall. Then she picked up her own pitchfork and returned to the work of cleaning manure out of Belle's stall.

Despite her reply, Stevie had to admit that her

brother was right, sort of. After the first thrill of being ungrounded had passed, she had quickly realized that the timing of their release was really bad. On the positive side, they had the next week off from school. But what good did that do them when none of their friends was around to help them celebrate? Lisa was in Los Angeles with her father. Callie and Scott were visiting their old hometown with their family. Carole was grounded and working her fingers to the bone with her volunteer group. Stevie's boyfriend, Phil, was in bed with a mild case of pneumonia.

"You know, this reeks," Stevie said with feeling as she stabbed violently at a pile of manure-stained straw with her pitchfork. "And I'm not talking about this stall, either."

"I know what you mean." Alex leaned on his pitchfork and gazed at his sister. "Why did everyone have to go away this week of all weeks?"

Stevie strongly suspected that by "everyone" Alex really meant "Lisa." She also guessed that the main reason he'd decided to hang out at Pine Hollow was because the stable reminded him of his girlfriend.

"I don't know," Stevie replied. She sighed, imagining for a moment how much fun she could have had in the next week if Phil hadn't been sick. Then she pushed the thought out of her mind. It was just too depressing. "Anyway, I was thinking of taking Belle out for a nice relaxing ride through the woods today. Want to come along?"

Alex wrinkled his nose. "A trail ride with my sister?" he said. "I don't know. I feel like enough of a loser as it is."

"Believe me, the idea doesn't thrill me, either," Stevie said sharply. "But we're stuck with each other, so we might as well make the most of it. Would you feel like less of a loser sitting around at home watching cartoons on TV with Michael?"

"It's a toss-up." Alex shrugged. "But anyway, why can't we make the most of it somewhere more interesting? We could catch that new action movie—I think it's playing at the mall."

"I don't want to see that. But I guess we could hit the mall if you want. Or we could go grab a slice at Pizza Manor," Stevie suggested halfheartedly. "Or a milk shake at TD's." She wasn't really hungry, but anything had to be better than standing around complaining all day. And she knew that Alex wasn't that excited about riding. He'd only taken it up because it gave him a chance to spend even more time with Lisa.

"I guess," Alex replied, sounding just as noncommittal as Stevie felt.

"Hi, Lakes!" a new voice broke in from down the aisle. "What are you two doing here? Does this mean the prison sentence is over?"

Stevie glanced over her shoulder and saw Deborah, Max's wife, heading toward them from the back entrance to the stable. That was a common shortcut that the whole Regnery family used to get into the stable, since their house stood on a hill just beyond the back paddocks.

"Hi, Deborah," Stevie said. "Yep, it's official. We've been paroled."

"Finally," Alex added, dropping his pitchfork against the wall and leaning against Belle's stall door.

Deborah smiled and pushed back her shoulder-length auburn hair. "That's great," she said. "Congratulations."

"Thanks," Alex said. He glanced at Stevie. "Hey, are we about done here? I'll take the wheel-barrow out back." Without waiting for an answer, he grabbed the handles and wheeled it off past Deborah, heading for the manure pit.

Meanwhile Stevie glanced behind Deborah, expecting to see one or both of her daughters trailing behind. "Where are the girls?"

"Oh, Maxi is following her father around, as usual. And Jeannie's taking a nap," Deborah reported. "There's a baby monitor in her room and the office, so I figured she'd be all right for a few minutes while I ran down here and looked up a few things."

Stevie was instantly on alert. Deborah was a successful reporter for one of the major dailies in nearby Washington, D.C. If she was looking up information at Pine Hollow . . . "Are you doing another story about horses?" Stevie asked eagerly.

Deborah grimaced. "Well, sort of," she said. "But don't get too excited—it's not another exposé or racetrack scandal." She sighed. "Not even close."

"What, then?" Stevie asked curiously, patting Belle as the mare nudged at her hair with her soft nose. She couldn't help noticing that Deborah didn't seem particularly fired up about her errand. That was strange—Deborah loved her job, and usually it showed.

Deborah sighed again. "It's sort of a human-interest piece," she said, reaching out to scratch Belle on the neck. "About retired show horses. Apparently there's some nice old lady up toward New Salisbury who takes in horses—boards them for owners who need to make room for their current mounts or whatever. She takes care of the retirees for the rest of their lives, gives them their medicines and so forth."

"That sounds nice," Stevie commented, releasing Belle from the cross-ties and leading her toward her stall. "It's good that those old horses have a place to go."

"No argument there," Deborah agreed, leaning against the stall's wide wooden doorway. "And I should probably be happy to give this service some

42

more publicity. It's just that it's not exactly *reporting*, you know?"

Stevie shrugged, not quite sure what Deborah was saying. "Okay, so maybe it's not exactly fast-breaking news." She gave Belle a pat and walked to the back of the stall to check her water bucket. "But somebody has to write those kinds of stories, right?"

"Right." Deborah frowned slightly and tugged at her thick auburn bangs. "It just seems that lately, that somebody is always me." She shot Stevie a quick glance and shrugged. "But don't mind me. I'm just feeling a little paranoid. Ever since my last maternity leave, I can't help wondering if the editors take me as seriously as they used to."

"Oh." Now Stevie understood, at least in part. Deborah's career meant a lot to her—Stevie could no more imagine Max's wife giving up reporting than she could picture Carole deciding she didn't like riding. "But those editors know you're great at what you do," she added as she gave Belle one last pat, stepped out of the stall, and latched the door behind her. "So what if you took a month or two off a couple of times? That doesn't mean you forgot everything you knew about reporting."

"You're right. It doesn't mean that." Deborah smiled. "Look, like I said, I'm probably just being a little oversensitive. And just because I may not be thrilled about this particular assignment, that doesn't mean I can blow it off. That's why I'm here doing my research."

Stevie thought Deborah's cheerful expression looked a little forced, but she figured it was better to let it drop. "Cool," she said. "What kind of stuff are you researching?"

"I'm not sure," Deborah said. "I figured I'd just take a look through some of Max's books and files and stuff for anything about senior show horses."

"Hmmm." Stevie blinked thoughtfully, trying to remember anything she'd ever read about the topic. "I'm not sure you'll find a whole lot of info on that there. Why don't you check the Internet instead?"

Deborah looked interested. "I tried that," she said. "I typed in *retired show horse* into a search engine, and ended up with nearly a million hits. I thought I'd do it the old-fashioned—"

"I've got a better idea," Stevie interrupted. "I just happen to know Carole's password. We can log into her account and check her file of favorite links." She grinned. "She has it categorized and cross-referenced so totally that even Lisa was impressed when she saw it."

Deborah laughed. "Well, I don't know," she said. "I appreciate the help, but I'm not sure hacking into someone else's files is good journalistic ethics."

Stevie waved one hand. "Oh, don't worry," she assured Deborah. "It's not like I sneaked a peek at the password when Carole wasn't looking. She gave it to Lisa and me so that we could use her horse info file whenever we need to." She grinned. "You know how Carole feels about educating everyone and anyone about horses."

"Oh. Well, in that case—"

"Yo," Alex broke in, loping down the aisle. "I left the wheelbarrow in the equipment shed. So are we going to ride or eat or what?"

"Neither." Stevie gestured at Deborah. "I need to help Deborah research her next Pulitzer Prize–winning article. So you'll have to entertain yourself for a while."

Alex actually looked disappointed. "Oh, well," he said. "Maybe I'll just head home. There's probably a game on TV or something."

"Okay. You can take the car if you want," Stevie offered, reaching into her jeans pocket for the keys. The twins had driven over to the stable in the battered blue two-door they shared, but it was only a ten-minute walk home from Pine Hollow.

Alex caught the keys as Stevie tossed them. "Thanks," he said. "I really . . ." His voice trailed off, and his eyes focused on a point somewhere past Stevie's right shoulder.

"What's wrong?" Turning to see what her

brother was looking at, Stevie saw Nicole Adams walking down the aisle toward them.

"Hi, guys!" Nicole sang out in her lilting, slightly breathy voice. She wriggled her fingers in a little wave.

Stevie returned the newcomer's smile weakly. She and Alex had gone to Fenton Hall with Nicole since kindergarten, but that didn't mean Stevie liked her much. For one thing, Nicole was friends with Veronica diAngelo and the rest of her snobby clique, and that alone was enough of a reason for Stevie to ignore her as much as possible. Besides, Nicole had never shown much interest in finding new girlfriends. She was too busy wowing the entire male population of the school with her pretty face, knockout figure, and flirtatious giggle.

*Of course, I never thought Alex would fall for any of that,* Stevie thought, sneaking a glance at her brother. *Even under the influence.* She shuddered as she remembered how Alex had slow danced with Nicole at that fateful party. True, he and Lisa had just broken up in front of everyone they knew. Also true, he'd had quite a few beers by that point. But still . . .

"What are you doing here, Nicole?" Alex asked. He smiled apologetically. "I mean, not that we're not happy to see you or whatever. But, well, what are you doing here?"

Nicole let out her famous giggle and tossed her

46

head. Her hair—a shade of pale, almost silvery blond that Stevie was quite sure didn't occur in nature—bounced around for a moment before settling into perfect waves just above her shoulders. "I'm looking for Denise McCaskill?" Nicole said. "I talked to her on the phone yesterday. I think she's the stable manager or something?"

"She is," Stevie confirmed. "I'm not sure where she is, though. Come to think of it, I haven't seen her since we got here." She glanced at her brother, who nodded his agreement without taking his eyes off Nicole.

"That's because she isn't here," Deborah put in. "She called in sick—some kind of nasty stomach bug, I think."

"Oh." Nicole looked disappointed. "Um, she said she'd talk to me about riding here."

"Don't worry." Stevie did her valiant best to hide her surprise. Nicole Adams riding at Pine Hollow? It just didn't compute. "I'm sure Max or Red can help you out. If you wander around a little, you're sure to run into one of them sooner or later."

"I've got a better idea," Alex said. He smiled at Nicole. "How about if I give you a little tour while you're looking for them? I mean, if you're looking for information on this place, I can probably help you out with the basics. I've been riding here for, like, almost a year."

47

Nicole smiled and briefly touched her fingers to his arm. "Thanks, Alex," she said. "That's so *sweet* of you."

Alex shrugged. "No big deal," he replied, looking very pleased with himself. "Come on, let's go."

Stevie watched the two of them amble off together down the aisle, chatting and laughing. "Yikes," she muttered, glad that Lisa wasn't around. She was sure her brother would never risk his relationship with his girlfriend just for a few minutes of flirtation with a party girl like Nicole. Still, it was perfectly obvious from the little exchange Stevie had just witnessed that Nicole had no problems flirting her bleach-blond head off with another girl's boyfriend. So it was just as well that Lisa was safely out of the state, where she couldn't accidentally come upon them and jump to the wrong conclusion.

*And it would definitely be the wrong conclusion,* Stevie assured herself, staring after the pair as they disappeared around the corner at the end of the aisle. *Alex would never be idiotic enough to mess things up again. Not after all the problems he and Lisa have had over the past couple of months . . .*

"What's wrong, Stevie?" Deborah asked. "You look weird. Are you sick? Maybe whatever Denise is out with is catching."

With a start, Stevie remembered the woman standing beside her. "Oh!" she said, pushing thoughts of Alex out of her head. He was a big boy—he had every right to hang out with Nicole if he wanted to, no matter what Stevie thought of her. "Um, nothing," she told Deborah. "Come on, let's go see what the World Wide Web has to tell us about retired show horses."

By the time the shrill chirp of Craig's whistle floated across the park, signaling the end of the workday, Carole's back was aching and her blisters were growing blisters. She groaned and stretched as the other volunteers started gathering up their tools and heading back toward the vans.

"Whew!" she said under her breath. "And I thought mucking out stalls and tossing hay was tiring." She felt a flash of sadness at the thought. Another day was ending—another day wasted, spent somewhere other than Pine Hollow. How much longer could she stand it?

As she headed across the playground, a light wind tickled her skin and she shivered slightly. She had been working so hard all afternoon that she hadn't noticed the growing chill creeping into the air. But now that the sun was sinking out of sight, the breeze that had felt so good as she worked made gooseflesh spring up on her skin.

Wrapping her arms around herself, Carole scurried for the van. Halfway there, one of the other volunteers—the young man with the wire-rimmed glasses—caught up with her. "Hi there," he said. "Listen, I wanted to tell you, my wife and I noticed how hard you were working today. Nice job. It's always good to have an enthusiastic newcomer on the team."

"Thanks," Carole said, struggling to remember the young man's name. Was he one of the people Dr. Durbin had introduced earlier?

The man smiled. "By the way, I don't think we've actually met yet. I'm Lionel." He pointed to the woman with the thick blond braid, who was talking to Dr. Durbin. "That's my wife, Nadine."

Carole smiled politely. "Nice to meet you," she said automatically. "I'm Carole."

"Are you a student, Carole?" Lionel asked.

"Uh-huh. I'm a junior at Willow Creek High." Carole was doing her best to seem interested in the conversation, but it wasn't easy. Now that she wasn't distracted by physical work, her mind kept returning to its constant preoccupation with how much she missed Starlight, Pine Hollow, and everything else having to do with horses and riding.

Lionel didn't seem to notice that anything was wrong. "Nadine and I really enjoy our work with Hometown Hope. We've tackled a few different projects with them since we moved here last year. All of them have been really satisfying. For instance, we helped repair and insulate some low-income homes after that big ice storm last winter.

50

And a couple of months ago, we got a bunch of businesses to donate paint and supplies so that we could repaint and renovate the barn over at the Free Rein riding place on the other side of town."

"Uh-huh." Carole forced herself to keep smiling, but Lionel's mention of Free Rein had hit her like a sharp blow to the gut. Was the whole world conspiring against her? Why was it that everywhere she turned, everything she saw or heard reminded her of what she'd lost? Her head throbbed, and she was afraid she was going to burst into tears.

Luckily, someone called to Lionel, and after a word of apology the young man hurried away.

Carole rubbed her eyes and sighed with relief. Now all she had to do was survive the van ride back across town. Then she could climb into her own car and treat herself to the only comfort her father couldn't take away: a good long cry.

# FOUR

"Baaaaaa!" Lily squealed delightedly, throwing her chubby little arms up over her head. "Baaaa-aaaaa!"

"Banana," Lisa said with a smile, breaking off another small piece of the fruit she was holding. "Can you say *banana*?"

Lily didn't answer. Instead, she leaned forward and crawled toward Lisa across the kitchen's white linoleum floor, stretching one hand toward the banana and almost tipping herself over to one side.

"Okay, okay, here you go." Lisa caught the baby and set her upright again, then handed her the gooey banana chunk. Lily shoved it into her mouth and chewed, looking very pleased with herself as she smeared banana glop across the front of her cheerful red corduroy playsuit.

Lisa smiled at her baby sister, glad that she'd finally been able to steal a few minutes alone with her. In the twenty-four hours since her arrival at her father's cozy Victorian cottage, she'd been bombarded almost nonstop with serious discussion about her college plans. Her father didn't seem to want to talk about anything else, and while Evelyn occasionally shot Lisa a sympathetic glance, she didn't seem eager to step in and change the subject. Not that she would have had much luck, probably, Lisa figured wryly. She was a little surprised that her father had actually allowed her to stop listening to his lectures long enough to sleep the night before. It had been a relief when he'd left the house half an hour earlier to go to the hardware store.

"Do you want another piece, Lily?" Lisa asked.

But Lily wasn't paying attention to Lisa—or the banana—anymore. She was staring over Lisa's shoulder, her eyes bright and eager. "Maaaaaaaaaa!" she exclaimed.

Lisa turned and saw her stepmother, Evelyn, coming through the back door with a bulging brown paper grocery bag in each arm. "Yes, that's right, little one," Evelyn crooned, dropping the bags on the counter. "Mama's here." She swooped forward and picked up the delighted baby, then turned to Lisa with a smile on her pretty, pixieish face. "Thanks for looking after her, Lisa. Believe me, grocery shopping is *much* easier when you don't have a curious baby trying to grab everything off the shelves as you pass."

"I can believe it," Lisa said with a laugh. "She

keeps me on my toes, that's for sure. I thought babies were supposed to sleep most of the day!"

Evelyn shifted Lily onto her other hip. "Not this baby," she said fondly, running one hand over Lily's soft, pale brown hair. "Her batteries never seem to run down. I think I'll go up and give her a bath now. That's usually the only thing that soothes her and makes her sleepy enough to want to take a nap."

"Can I help?" Lisa offered.

"That's okay." Evelyn shrugged and smiled. "You've seen how tiny our bathroom is. I'm not sure both of us could fit in there at the same time. Besides, you've been so much help already. You deserve a few minutes to relax."

*Before Dad gets back and jumps on my case again,* Lisa finished in her head, guessing that was approximately what her stepmother was thinking. "Thanks," she told Evelyn. "But before I start relaxing, I'll take care of the groceries, okay?"

"That would be great," Evelyn said. "Thanks, Lisa. You're a lifesaver."

"No problem." Lisa set to work as Evelyn disappeared up the stairs with Lily. It only took her a few minutes to unload the grocery bags and put everything away. That left her with a rare moment of quiet—probably the first waking one she'd had since arriving in California, aside from her shower that morning.

Her first thought was the English paper she had due when she returned from break. But she quickly pushed that idea aside. She would have plenty of time to finish her homework on the flight home. She considered calling some of the friends she'd made over the summer at her job working on the set of *Paradise Ranch*. But she felt a little weird about that. She'd been really close to those people when she'd seen them every day. But even though she'd planned to keep in touch with several of them, it had never quite happened. The only person from the show she'd talked to since then was Skye—which made sense, since he'd been her friend for years.

Thinking about Skye, as always, made her feel a twinge of uneasiness as her thoughts turned to Alex. But that gave her another idea. Maybe she should call Alex and Stevie. The night before, Alex had called to give her the good news that the twins were finally ungrounded.

*What a bizarre thought,* Lisa thought with a slight smile. *It's been a long time since I could just pick up the phone and call Alex or Stevie whenever I felt like it. Too bad it has to be long distance, all the way from California.*

Still, she was sure her father wouldn't really mind the extra charges. She hadn't been able to talk to Alex for long the previous evening because he hadn't managed to reach her until she'd returned from dinner out with her father, Evelyn, and Lily. It had only been eight-thirty in California, but that meant in Willow Creek it was already eleven-thirty, and Mr. and Mrs. Lake had insisted that Alex keep the call short.

Hurrying over to the phone on the wall beside the refrigerator, she quickly punched in the familiar number. But all she got was a busy signal.

"Rats," she muttered as she hung up. There was nothing to do but wait and try again in a few minutes—and hope her father didn't return before she had a chance to unload her frustrations on either her boyfriend or one of her other best friends. She wished she could call Carole, but she knew better than to try. Colonel Hanson was a fun-loving, easygoing guy most of the time. But as a former Marine, he believed strongly in discipline when a situation called for it. There was no way he was going to make an exception to his no-phone-calls rule, even for a call from California.

As Lisa was trying to figure out how long she should wait before trying the Lakes' number again, the phone rang, startling her.

*Maybe that's Stevie or Alex calling now,* she thought hopefully, grabbing the receiver before the phone could ring a second time. *Maybe they read my mind and knew I needed to talk.*

"Hello?" she said eagerly. "Lisa Atwood speaking."

"Lisa?" The voice sounded confused. Confused and familiar.

"Peter?" Lisa could hardly believe her ears. "Is that you?" She could barely remember the last time she'd heard her older brother's voice. He had been living in Europe since graduating from college several years earlier. After spending some time in England, Japan, and Africa, he had recently moved to Switzerland, where he had a job translating product labels into various languages for foreign sales.

"It's me," Peter confirmed. "How are you doing, little sis?"

"Fine," Lisa replied automatically. For a moment she had the urge to spill all her problems to her brother. He would understand what she was going through with their parents if anyone would. After all, he was the one who'd surprised the whole family with the announcement that he'd won a scholarship to a college in Texas, and that he was going there instead of to their father's alma mater, the University of Virginia, as Mr. and Mrs. Atwood had expected. Then a couple of years later, Peter had informed his parents that he was transferring to a school in England to study languages. He had also clashed with them over his choice of careers—first about wanting to stay in Europe rather than returning home and settling down, then regarding his dreams of being a writer. His parents had won out on the second question—at least partly. After a stint as a research assistant in Africa, Peter had gotten a series of steady jobs all over Europe, most of them making use of his fluency in French, German, Japanese, Swedish, and of course English.

*Still, maybe he* wouldn't *understand that well,* Lisa thought. *After all, getting that first scholarship was a good thing—even Mom and Dad realized that. And for all the rest of it, he was so far away that it hardly mattered what they thought. I mean, it seems like he's hardly been in the same state or country with any of us for more than a few days at a time since he graduated from high school.*

Pushing aside a flash of regret and sadness at that thought, Lisa clutched the phone tighter, not wanting to miss this chance to talk with her brother. "So how are you?" she asked. "Are you at home or at work? This connection is so clear! It sounds like you're calling from next door, not all the way from Switzerland."

"Well, actually, there's a reason for that," Peter said. "I'm not in Switzerland. I'm right here in L.A."

Lisa gasped, not sure she'd heard him correctly. "What!" she exclaimed. "What do you mean? Nobody told me you were coming!"

"Nobody knows. I just flew in—I'm at the airport. Surprise!"

58

"Wow. I'm definitely surprised." Lisa leaned against the kitchen counter for support. Suddenly she felt a twinge of suspicion. "Wait a minute," she said. "Dad didn't ask you to come, did he? I mean, to talk to me about college, you know, like calling in the reinforcements."

"Huh?" Peter sounded genuinely confused. "What do you mean? Dad doesn't know I'm here at all. Remember? I just told you, nobody knows. What do you mean, reinforcements?"

"Um, never mind." Lisa laughed sheepishly. "I'll tell you when you get here."

"Okay. And I'll have something to tell you, too. Actually, it's kind of a big surprise. For the whole family, I mean."

"A big surprise?" Lisa repeated. "What is it?"

"Later," Peter insisted. "You'll see."

Lisa frowned. She hadn't spoken much to her brother lately, but she knew she couldn't be imagining the nervous tone in his voice. What was going on? What kind of surprise would make him fly all the way from Europe to see them?

Still, she figured she could wait a little longer to find out. After all, it was only a short drive to Mr. Atwood's house from the airport. "Well, all right," she told her brother. "But you'd better get here as fast as an L.A. cab can drive you. I'm in total suspense."

"Well, I'm not sure we—that is, I can't promise

I'll be there right away," Peter replied. "Actually, it will probably be a couple of hours at least. Is Dad there now?"

"No, but he'll be back soon," Lisa replied. "But what do you mean, it will take you hours to get here? What are you planning to do, walk?"

"No, nothing like that. There's just something I need to do first." Peter's voice sounded nervous again. "Um, and by the way, maybe you shouldn't tell Dad I called. Now that I think about it, it might be better to just surprise him in person."

"Okay, if that's what you want." Lisa shrugged, still mystified by her brother's weird comments. What could he possibly have to do in L.A. that would keep him from arriving for hours? "You're just lucky I was here to pick up the phone, though."

"I know. And I'm sorry I can't tell you more. It's just that I don't want to go ahead and— Well, never mind. All I can say now is, I think you'll be more excited about my surprise than anyone."

"Really?" That made Lisa more curious than ever. But she decided that if her brother wanted to keep his secret a little longer, she would respect that. "Okay, then, I won't breathe a word. See you in a while."

"Thanks, Lisa. See you."

*What was that all about?* Lisa wondered as she hung up the phone. *Peter usually isn't the mysterious type. And what did he mean when he said I would be more excited than anyone else about his surprise?*

She wandered out to the sun-dappled back porch and flopped onto a lounge chair, still thinking about her brother's unexpected call.

Suddenly she had an idea. *Maybe this has something to do with his old dreams of being a screenwriter,* she thought. *I thought he gave up on the idea of writing for the movies, but maybe he's just been keeping quiet about it. Maybe he has a script ready, and he's here in L.A. shopping it around to producers and stuff.*

Lisa sat up straighter in her chair. Her screenwriting theory had begun as an idle thought, but now she wondered if she might actually be on to something. Peter had been pretty gung ho for a while about writing film scripts. Was it really so outlandish to think that he might still be trying to make his old dream come true?

With a shrug, she sank back in the chair again. No doubt about it, it would be pretty cool if Peter was on the verge of screenwriting stardom. But there was no sense getting all worked up about it—she would just have to wait until he arrived to find out the truth.

*In the meantime,* she thought, letting her eyes close and enjoying the warm California sunshine on her face, *I'll just think about how great it will be to have something other than my college plans to oc-cupy Dad's attention for a while.*

"What do you say, Belle?" Stevie opened her horse's stall door and stepped inside. "Feel like let-ting me play around with your mane? A little extra braiding practice never hurts, right?"

The friendly mare came forward with a snort to greet her owner. She snuffled at Stevie's pockets, obviously hoping for a treat. Instead, Stevie pulled out a mane comb and a handful of rubber bands.

Belle cast a suspicious dark brown eye at the equipment. Then she tossed her head and let out another snort.

"Okay, okay." Stevie rubbed the mare's soft nose. "I know I've groomed you, like, three times today already, but give me a break, okay? It's either this, or Max thinks I'm slacking and makes me muck out stalls—again."

Stevie sighed. Spending all day at the stable, for the first time since before that party that had got-ten her grounded, should have been a dream come true. She was finally free to do whatever she wanted, she had a whole week off from school—what could be better than putting in some serious quality time with her horse?

But as much as Stevie loved having all the time in the world to spend with Belle, she was starting to realize that a big part of what she loved about hanging out at Pine Hollow was the people who were usually there. It just didn't seem like the same place without Carole, Lisa, Callie, and Phil to share it with.

"Not that I'm complaining, of course," she told Belle, stroking her glossy copper-colored neck. "Not really. This still beats being grounded, that's for sure."

"Talking to the stock again, Lake?" a familiar voice came from the direction of the aisle. "How many times do I have to tell you that horses don't speak English?"

Stevie glanced up at Max, who was gazing at her over the half door of Belle's stall, and grinned. "Oh, I believe you, Max," she said. "But you're going to have to convince Belle. She definitely understands when I say the word *carrot.*"

In response, Belle's ears, which had been tipping lazily to the sides, suddenly pricked forward alertly. The mare let out a snort and lowered her nose to one of Stevie's hands, then to the other, clearly searching for the treat her owner had mentioned.

Stevie laughed, and Max let out a chuckle. "All right, all right," he said with mock gruffness. "Leave it to you to be the exception to yet another rule, Stevie. In any case, if you're finished conversing with your horse, I could use your help."

"Sure, Max," Stevie said immediately. "What do you need?"

If Max was surprised at her eagerness, he didn't let it show. "Judy's here to float Eve's teeth, and you know how Eve feels about adults, especially when it comes to her mouth." He stroked his chin. "I thought we'd try having a couple of her favorite nonadults around this time and see if it helps."

Stevie nodded. Eve was now such a beloved, healthy Pine Hollow horse that it was easy to forget she had been abused and badly neglected by her former owners. The only evidence that remained of the gentle mare's early days were a few faded scars around her ankles and a lingering unease around some adults, particularly men. She especially hated having any adult—even a gentle, frequently seen female adult like Judy Barker, the local equine vet—poke around in her mouth.

"Sure thing. I'm right behind you," Stevie said. She gave Belle a quick pat, then let herself out of the stall and hurried down the aisle after Max.

When the two of them turned the corner into the other arm of the U-shaped stable aisle, Stevie saw that Judy already had Eve in cross-ties outside her stall. She was stroking the mare's face gently and chatting with Kitty Asher, one of the newest members of the beginner riding class. The soft-spoken eight-year-old was patting Eve on one silvery-gray shoulder, and the mare was clearly enjoying the attention.

"Hi, Stevie," Judy said when she spotted the new arrivals. "So Max corralled you into being another dental assistant, huh? Do you know Kitty?"

"Sure." Stevie smiled at the younger girl. She'd met her a few times during preparations for the horse show, when the beginning and intermediate riders had all been eager to help Stevie and the other competitors. "How's it going, Kitty Kat?"

Kitty giggled shyly. "Pretty good, Stevie Evie." She giggled again and pointed to the mare. "Stevie, Evie. Get it?"

Stevie laughed. "Good one." She stepped up to Eve and patted her on the cheek. "And how are you, sweetie?"

The horse didn't respond, but Max cleared his throat. "All right, then," he said. "Before Stevie gets into some long-winded conversation with the patient, why don't we get started?"

"Sounds good to me," Judy said with a smile. She glanced at Stevie. "Want to hold her head? Kitty, you could help out by standing right over here." She pointed to a spot off to one side, which would be in Eve's line of vision. "That way she'll be able to see that you're here, and that will help keep her calm, but you'll be out of the line of fire if it doesn't work."

"Okay," Kitty said, moving into position.

Stevie stepped to Eve's head and took hold of her halter. "It's going to be okay, Evie," she crooned to the horse. "Don't worry about a thing. Judy's a totally painless dentist." She noticed out of the corner of her eye that Max had moved back out of Eve's line of sight.

When everyone was in place, Judy started pulling equipment out of her battered black medical bag. The first item she removed was a shiny steel contraption with leather straps.

"What's that?" Kitty asked, her eyes wide.

"It's called a speculum," Judy told the little girl. "It will keep Eve's mouth open while I work. Otherwise she might try to bite me, especially if she's nervous."

Stevie nodded. "Judy uses the same contraption on my horse, Belle," she told Kitty. "Have you ever seen a horse get its teeth floated before?"

Kitty shook her head. "I don't even know what that means," she admitted.

"It's an important part of routine care," Judy explained as she pried Eve's mouth open and, with Stevie's help, got the speculum in place. "Horses need to have their teeth filed smooth—we call it floating—once or twice a year. Otherwise they end up with sharp spots, especially on the outside upper teeth and inside lower ones, because of the way the teeth rub together when they chew."

Kitty nodded, glancing at Eve curiously. "That would poke them in the mouth."

"Right." Judy pulled out her dental float. "And if it hurts them to chew the normal way, the horse might decide to chew with an up-and-down motion instead of the usual side-to-side grinding movement. And we all know what that can lead to, right, Stevie?"

"Huh?" Stevie had started to tune out Judy's lecture, but now she snapped back to attention. "Um, sure. If they don't chew their food right, it can give them colic and stuff."

Max rolled his eyes. "Would you care to define 'and stuff,' Stevie?"

Stevie grinned. Max never missed an opportunity to teach. In this case, the primary pupil was certainly Kitty, who was hanging on every word. But Stevie was sure that Max also wanted to make sure Stevie knew the facts.

"Sure, Max," Stevie replied. "If there's a wad of grass or hay that isn't chewed up all the way, it sort of moves down the horse's throat in a wad. If it gets stuck in the esophagus, it's called choke. And if it makes it farther down and can't be digested right, it means impaction colic, which can require surgery."

Judy glanced up from her work, looking impressed. "That's right, Stevie. One of the signs is quidding, when bits of partly chewed food fall out of the horse's mouth while she's eating. And the problems can be worse in older horses whose teeth are in poor shape. Eve is only nine years old or so, which means we just have to keep up with her usual dental work. But a lot of older horses—like Chip and Nickel, for instance—need extra attention to keep their teeth healthy and strong."

As the words left Judy's mouth, Eve suddenly decided she'd had enough of the file, the speculum, and all the rest of it. With a loud snort, the mare yanked her head out of Judy's grip. Before Stevie could tighten her grip, the halter slipped through her fingers and Eve began to rear.

Max stepped forward quickly, catching the mare's mane and pulling her down before she could stretch the cross-ties to their limit. But his presence seemed to excite her more, and she snorted and danced nervously in place, showing the whites of her eyes.

*Eve sees Max every day,* Stevie thought, amazed as she often was at how deeply ingrained some equine behavior could be. *And by this time, she knows he's not going to hurt her. But I guess right now, he's just another man to her. Just like the man or men who hurt her when she was younger.*

A quiet voice interrupted the scene. "Need some help?"

Stevie glanced past Eve and saw that Ben was heading toward them. Without waiting for an answer from any of the assembled humans, he walked straight up to Eve and put one hand on her muzzle. "Hey," he murmured. "It's okay, Eve. Everything's going to be all right, okay? I promise." He took hold of the halter, and Max released his grip and stepped back.

Stevie held her breath. For a moment, Eve continued to snort and stomp her feet. But as Ben continued to whisper soothingly to her, her ears pricked toward him and her eyes stopped rolling. Within a matter of seconds, she was standing quietly once again, only her rapidly swishing tail revealing her agitation.

Judy let out a low whistle. "Good work, Ben," she said. "Want to stick around while I finish up here?"

Ben nodded, and Judy got back to work. Stevie just stood and watched, amazed at what Ben had done. Glancing over at Max, who was rubbing his arm, Stevie shook her head slightly. *Eve was so worked up and scared that she was even terrified of Max,* she thought. *And yet Ben still managed to get through to her. That's something. That's really something.*

Kitty seemed to be thinking the same thing. She sidled over to stand beside Stevie, though her wide brown eyes never left Ben and Eve. "Wow," the little girl whispered. "Eve really likes him, huh?"

"Yeah, I guess she does," Stevie whispered back.

With Ben's help, Eve's dental work was soon finished. As Ben unhooked the mare from her cross-ties, Stevie wandered off toward Belle's stall, still feeling in awe of Ben's abilities. *You know, it's times like these that I sort of, maybe, see why Carole thinks Ben's so special.* She smiled to herself, thinking of how shy her friend could be when it came to guys—especially certain dark-eyed, brooding, horse-crazy guys. *Not that she would admit that it's anything more than purely professional admiration, of course.*

As she rounded the corner of the stable aisle, Stevie saw George Wheeler coming toward her. George was a pudgy, pale, thoroughly unathletic-looking guy who was in Stevie's grade at Fenton Hall. He also happened to be one of the best riders at Pine Hollow. When he was in the saddle, all his bumbling awkwardness fell away and he seemed to become one with his horse. On his own two feet, however, he was basically a hopeless nerd—nice enough, but pretty inept, especially when it came to girls. Stevie knew that George had a big crush on Callie, though he claimed that the two of them were just friends. She guessed Callie's trip to the West Coast with her family was the most likely reason for the glum look on George's face at the moment.

"Hi," Stevie greeted him. "How's it going?"

George shrugged. "Okay, I guess." He couldn't

manage to put much feeling into his words, though. In fact, he looked downright depressed.

*Wow,* Stevie thought as she nodded and continued down the aisle past him. *I wonder if Callie knows how bad he still has it for her? Maybe I'd better give her a heads-up when she gets back. Then again, maybe it's none of my business. After all, Callie's a big girl, and she can take care of herself. . . .*

Before Stevie could think much more about that, she heard the sound of laughter coming from a nearby stall. Wandering over to investigate, she looked over the half door and saw her brother and Nicole Adams inside. They were trying to lift a saddle onto the high, broad back of Congo, who was usually one of Pine Hollow's calmest and most reliable school horses. Today, however, he seemed to be in a mischievous mood. Every time Alex lifted the saddle up, the horse took a step sideways. Stevie was sure it didn't help that Nicole kept letting out high-pitched giggles every time the horse moved.

"Hey, guys," Stevie said.

Alex glanced over at her. "Oh, hi, Stevie," he said. "I didn't know you were still here."

*Is it my imagination, or does he sound a little guilty?* Stevie thought. She glanced at Nicole, who gazed back with wide, innocent blue eyes.

"We were just getting ready to go for a trail ride," Nicole said. "Do you want to come?"

71

"No thanks," Stevie replied automatically. "I already took Belle out today."

"Okay," Nicole said.

*Is it my imagination,* Stevie thought, *or does she look kind of relieved that I said no?*

She said good-bye and moved off toward Belle's stall, feeling a little disturbed by what she'd just seen. But really, what was the big deal? Her brother was just hanging out with Nicole because he was bored while Lisa was away. Right?

*Definitely right,* she told herself. *Alex loves Lisa. He's so crazy about her that it probably hasn't even occurred to him that anyone could ever suspect that anything might be going on between him and Nicole. There's no way he'd even say hello to her if he thought Lisa might not like it. No way.*

Still, an anxious knot twisted in her stomach when she imagined what Lisa might think if she came across her boyfriend and Nicole laughing together the way they were now. Would she be jealous? Hurt? Angry?

Stevie had no idea. It was hard to remember what it felt like to be uncertain about a relationship. She and Phil had been together for so long that it seemed downright silly to get all worked up if he talked to another girl.

*I'm sure Lisa's way past all that jealousy stuff by now, too, especially after that ridiculous business with Skye this summer. She knows Alex would never do*

72

*anything to hurt her or mess up their relationship,* Stevie thought as she reached out to pat Belle, who had stuck her head out to greet her. Stevie patted her horse absently, glancing over her shoulder toward Congo's stall. *Still, it probably wouldn't hurt to mention that to Nicole the next time an opportunity presents itself.*

# FIVE

Carole was scraping crusty old paint off the park's creaky wooden seesaw when Dr. Durbin approached her. "Well now, how's everything going, Carole?" the vice principal asked cheerfully. "What do you think of our project so far?"

"It's fine," Carole replied politely, lowering her scraper and wiping her brow. Despite the cool, crisp fall weather, the hard work was keeping her warm. "Very interesting."

Dr. Durbin laughed. "Don't give me that. Picking up other people's garbage isn't anybody's idea of a party. But it's got to be done, and that's why we do it."

"Um, right," Carole said. She glanced over at several neighborhood residents, who were helping Craig carry off some overstuffed garbage bags. Nearby, a small group of teenagers were talking and laughing loudly as they scraped gum off a couple of the park's benches. One of them had brought a portable CD player, which was adding to the general din. Dr. Durbin might not think it was a party, but the people who lived in the neighborhood of the park seemed to be turning it into one. More than a dozen locals had come out to help so far that day, some staying for just a few minutes and others putting in long hours of work along with the Hometown Hope volunteers.

But there was one local resident Carole couldn't help looking for. So far she hadn't seen any sign of Ben, but that didn't stop her from checking out each newcomer and passerby to see if it was him.

*Like there's any chance he'd be hanging around here,* she thought as Dr. Durbin leaned over to flick a large paint chip off the seesaw's wooden handle. *I'm sure he's over at Pine Hollow right now, putting in a few extra hours on his day off, as usual.*

"In any case, that's what Hometown Hope is all about," Dr. Durbin said, obviously not noticing Carole's distraction. "Making things better however we can."

"Uh-huh." Just then Carole saw a group of children crossing the street and heading toward the park. She recognized most of them from the day before. However, the little girl with the dark eyes wasn't among them, and Carole found herself oddly disappointed. There was something about that little girl . . .

"Excuse me a minute," she told Dr. Durbin.

"Um, I want to go say hi to those kids." She hurried toward them.

They gazed at her cautiously as she approached. "Who are you?" said a skinny boy wearing a faded Washington Redskins T-shirt.

"My name's Carole," Carole replied with a smile. "I saw you guys here yesterday, so I thought I'd come say hi. Do you live around here?"

Several of the children nodded, while the others just continued to stare at her. "I live in that green house," a girl with glasses volunteered, pointing across the street at a tired-looking but neatly maintained single-family house on a tiny lot.

"That looks like a nice house." Carole smiled at her, then glanced around at the others. "But one of you is missing," she went on. "Where is she?"

"Where's who?" the skinny boy asked, crossing his arms over his chest.

"You know, your friend who was with you yesterday," Carole prompted. She held up one hand. "She's about this tall, with curly dark hair. . . ."

Another little boy's eyes lit up. "Oh!" he said. "You mean Zani. She's not here."

A girl with freckles nodded solemnly. "Zani can't play as much ever since her gramps hurt his leg."

"That's too bad," Carole said. "How did her gramps get hurt?"

Before the kids could answer, Carole spied another figure walking across the street in their direction. With a gasp, she recognized Ben. Suddenly all the embarrassment, confusion, and pain of the Saturday two weeks before flooded back, as fresh and raw as if it had just happened.

The children were talking again, but she hardly heard them. Time seemed to slide into some kind of weird slow motion as she watched Ben approach the park, his dark eyes on the ground, a shock of dark hair falling forward over his face. Carole was so startled to see him in the flesh, even after her earlier thoughts, that it took her a moment to notice that he was holding the little dark-eyed girl—Zani—by the hand.

*Huh?* Carole thought blankly, not comprehending what she was seeing. *What's he doing with her?* Then she recalled the time she'd followed Ben home and seen that tired-looking old man in the yard. At the time, she'd assumed that the old man was Ben's grandfather. Could he also be the "gramps" the kids were talking about? Could Ben and Zani be siblings?

*He never mentioned having any brothers or sisters,* Carole thought, her gaze still glued to Ben, who hadn't looked up long enough to notice her. *Then again, Ben doesn't mention a whole lot that doesn't have to do with horses.*

Just then Ben finally glanced ahead and noticed the activity at the park. He stopped in the middle of the street, frowning and looking surprised and almost angry. His dark eyes swept the place, and he looked undecided as Zani tugged at his hand, trying to move him toward her friends.

Before she knew what she was doing, Carole took a step in their direction. Maybe this was her chance to talk to him—to find out what was going on between them. In fact, it could be her only chance.

Feeling nervous but determined, she took a deep breath and another step. But at that moment Ben suddenly moved again. He turned abruptly on his heel and strode back across the street in the direction he'd come, dragging Zani along beside him.

Carole stood stock-still, her face flaming. Had Ben seen her? She thought she'd seen his gaze flicker toward her just before he'd turned and left. But if that was true . . .

She couldn't finish the thought. Her breath was coming in sharp, ragged gasps. Her head spun, and for a second she was genuinely afraid she might pass out.

"Hey, Carole," Lionel called at that moment, hurrying toward her with a hammer in his hand. "Could you help us out over here for a sec? We can't get this board in position—we need one more person to help hold it."

Carole couldn't seem to get her mouth and brain working together well enough to respond.

She couldn't even manage to turn and look at Lionel. Instead, she whirled around and raced toward the far side of the park where the vans were parked, ignoring his surprised calls. Seconds later she was behind one of the big white vehicles, her back pressed to its cool, hard side. Her shoulders heaving, she did her best to regain control of herself. But it was a long time before her hands stopped shaking enough for her to return to work.

"Another thing for you to consider, Lisa," Mr. Atwood said as he took his place at the kitchen table between his wife and Lily. "What about the cost of keeping a car at college with you? You wouldn't need one at most of the other schools on your list, but I assume you would probably want one at NVU. Have you thought about that extra cost?"

Lisa bit back a sigh as she slipped her napkin onto her lap and picked up her fork. Couldn't her father let his lecture rest, even during dinner? "Yes, as a matter of fact I have. Was the grocery store crowded today, Evelyn?" she asked, pointedly changing the subject.

"Not too bad," Evelyn replied lightly with a worried glance at Mr. Atwood. "I guess everybody's saving their Thanksgiving shopping till the last minute. Or maybe they did it already. It takes all kinds, I guess, right?"

Lisa recognized that her stepmother was babbling, and she guessed that she hated the thought of spending another meal listening to her husband's nonstop college lecture almost as much as Lisa did. *So then why doesn't she tell Dad to ease up?* Lisa thought with a flash of irritation. *I mean, would it kill her to back me up a little once in a while?*

At that moment there was a knock on the door. "Anybody home?" her brother's voice called from the front of the house.

Mr. Atwood almost choked on the water he was sipping. "Peter?" he cried in disbelief. Hopping up from his seat, he hurried toward the doorway. "Son? Is that you?"

Peter appeared in the doorway just in time to meet his father heading out. "Dad!" he cried with a grin, clapping Mr. Atwood on the back. "Surprise!"

Lisa pushed back her chair with a smile as her father grabbed her brother's hand and pumped it up and down, almost sputtering as he tried to figure out what was going on. *I don't blame him,* she thought. *If I didn't already know he was coming, I'd probably be acting like Daffy Duck right now myself.*

She walked over, giving her father and brother a moment to finish their greeting. While she waited for her turn, she drank in the sight of her brother. She hadn't seen him since the previous Christmas, but as always, his face was so familiar that it was almost eerie. Peter had their father's straight, thin brown hair and their mother's aquiline nose and wide-set brown eyes. His fingers were long and finely boned, just like Lisa's own.

*I can't believe he's really here,* she thought. *Talk about a pleasant surprise! Not to mention perfect timing as a handy distraction.*

She pushed aside all thoughts of college and never-ending lectures as her brother turned to her. Stepping toward her for a hug, Peter winked. "Thanks for not blowing the surprise, sis," he murmured into her hair as he squeezed her tight.

"No problem," Lisa whispered back.

After greeting Evelyn politely and stooping down long enough to kiss Lily on the forehead, Peter stepped back and waved his hand at someone who had just opened the front door and walked into the hallway. "Now, before you start asking all kinds of questions about why I'm here, please allow me to introduce someone," he said.

Lisa looked at her brother in surprise. *I didn't know anyone was with him,* she thought. *He didn't mention anything like that on the phone. Maybe it's one of those movie producers I was daydreaming about earlier. . . .*

But the woman who stepped into the room in response to Peter's wave didn't look like a movie producer. In fact, she looked an awful lot like a rider. Her smooth, coffee-colored hair was pulled back in a severe ponytail at the nape of her neck, and she was wearing jodhpurs and a long-sleeved white shirt. Her pale blue eyes, the most noticeable feature in her tanned, unsmiling face, swept the room, taking them all in. Lisa thought the woman must be somewhere in her late twenties or early thirties, making her just a few years older than Peter.

"Greta, I'd like you to meet my family," Peter announced, gesturing to them each in turn. "This is my father, Richard Atwood, and his wife, Evelyn. That's my little sister, Lisa, over there. And of course, my even littler half sister, Lily."

"*Guten Tag,*" Greta said. "Hello."

Judging by the German, Greta wasn't a local producer. She must have come with Peter from Switzerland, where German was one of the four main languages. But why was she here? For that matter, why was Peter here? Lisa was starting to get the impression that this wasn't just an impromptu Thanksgiving visit.

Peter glanced around at his family and took a deep breath. Then, putting one hand around Greta's shoulders, he smiled rather nervously. "Family, I'd like you to meet Greta. Greta Atwood."

Lisa frowned. For one crazy moment, she

thought maybe Peter had discovered some long-lost cousin over in Europe.

Then another possibility hit her with the force of a freight train. Judging by her father's loud gasp, she guessed he'd just had the same thought. "Greta Atwood," Mr. Atwood repeated. "What do you mean? You two aren't—"

"Yep!" Peter replied, pulling Greta a little closer. "We made it official day before yesterday when we flew into Las Vegas. We're married!"

"Married," Lisa repeated numbly, staring from her brother to the stranger by his side and then back again. She vaguely noticed that Greta still hadn't cracked a smile, though she did look interested in the family's reactions. "You're serious? You're married?"

"For better, for worse, for richer, for poorer, and all that good stuff," Peter replied with strained cheerfulness. "So, what do you think? Aren't you going to congratulate us?"

"Congratulations," Evelyn said politely. "Um, you'll have to excuse us, Peter—er, and Greta. I think we're all a little taken aback by this."

Mr. Atwood didn't speak. Lisa didn't have to try to imagine how stunned he was. She was feeling the same way herself.

Peter cleared his throat and took a step farther into the room, pulling Greta with him. "Hey, listen, sorry I didn't tell you sooner," he said. "I mean, it was really kind of a spur-of-the-moment thing, you know? We didn't plan to elope or anything. But when Greta told me she was coming to the States for business—" He glanced at Lisa. "By the way, she's a horse broker. She's bought and sold horses for all kinds of sports and stuff all over Europe."

"Yes, that is correct," Greta put in. "My family has been involved in horses for several generations."

"Anyway," Peter went on, "I figured it would be a good excuse to come along and see everyone. She had to go to Vegas, and when we got there, well, the moment just seemed right. You know?"

Lisa didn't know what to say, and the rest of the family was equally speechless. Her big brother— married? Without telling anyone? It just didn't compute. Peter was usually so sensible, so methodical and careful. What had gotten into him?

Peter cleared his throat. "Um, there's one more thing," he said. "Greta—er, that is, *we*—have two children. I mean, they were her children, and now that we're married . . . Well, you get the picture." He grinned sheepishly. "They're waiting in the rental car—we thought it might be better that way." He squeezed Greta's shoulder. "*Liebchen,* why don't you go bring them in now?"

"Yes, I will go get Hanni and Dieter," Greta

declared. She nodded briskly at the Atwoods and strode out of the room.

Lisa slumped against the edge of the table as Mr. Atwood started shooting questions at Peter. *Wow,* she thought, still stunned by her brother's announcement. *I guess it's safe to say I won't be hearing anything more about college anytime soon!*

# SIX

The next morning at the park, Carole was struggling to shove a large piece of moldy, smelly, damp cardboard into a too-small garbage bag when she felt a pair of warm hands clap over her eyes from behind.

"Surprise!" a very familiar voice sang out. "Guess who?"

"Stevie!" Carole exclaimed, dropping the cardboard, knocking her friend's hands away, and spinning around. She was so happy to see Stevie that she couldn't resist throwing her arms around her in a tight hug. "Hi! What are you doing here?"

Stevie hugged her in return, then grinned at her. "Well, we never got to celebrate your birthday last week, since we were both grounded." She shrugged. "So I figured, hey, at least today *one* of us isn't grounded. So I thought I'd come by, wish you a belated happy birthday, and hang out for a while."

"Cool." Carole couldn't believe how great it was

to see Stevie. She'd missed her friends even more than she'd realized. Suddenly remembering where they were, she shot an anxious glance at Dr. Durbin, who was trimming some overgrown bushes nearby. "But I'm not sure the people here are going to like it if you just hang. You'll have to do some work if you want to stay."

"No biggie." Stevie flexed her biceps playfully. "After all those extra chores Mom and Dad made me do while I was grounded, Manual Labor is my middle name."

Noticing that Craig was looking over at them curiously, Carole quickly gathered up the cardboard again. "Grab that plastic bag, will you?" she said. "We have to cram this in there somehow."

"Got it," Stevie said agreeably. "So, how's this whole volunteer thing going, anyway? Lisa told me about it the other day."

Carole nodded. She had filled Lisa in on her punishment the previous week at school. "It's going okay," she said. "Well, you know. As okay as it could be."

Stevie shot her a sympathetic glance, but she didn't say anything. The two girls worked in silence for a couple of minutes. Finally they managed to get the cardboard bagged up. Carole tossed it onto the pile of garbage bags nearby, then brushed off her hands and returned to Stevie.

"Okay," she said. "I think I'm supposed to be on raking duty next. Want to join me?"

"You got it," Stevie replied.

The two of them grabbed rakes from the supply area and set to work on a rough section of dusty path, raking away scraps of debris and smoothing out the surface. "So what's been going on at Pine Hollow since I've been gone?" Carole asked. "Tell me everything. How's Starlight? Did the grain company remember the new order this time? How's the intermediate class doing with the bandaging Max has been teaching them?"

Stevie held up her hands, laughing. "Hold it!" she exclaimed. "How do you expect me to answer all those questions if you never shut up?"

Carole grinned sheepishly. "Sorry," she said. "So?"

"Much better." Stevie smiled and started filling her in on the activities at the stable over the past week. When she finished, Carole sighed with a mixture of relief and sadness. It sounded as though everything was running smoothly. But hearing about daily life at the stable made her miss being there even more, if that was possible.

"So what about you?" she asked wistfully. "It must be great to be ungrounded. You can hang out at Pine Hollow all day, go for a ride whenever you want. . . ."

"True, sort of," Stevie said. "Actually, though, I

realized it's not quite as much fun without all my favorite people there. I mean, you're grounded. Lisa and Callie are off doing the West Coast Thanksgiving thing. Phil's still flat on his back with pneumonia." She wrinkled her nose. "I've actually been forced to hang out with my twin, if you can believe that."

Carole smiled. She could believe it very well. Stevie and Alex hadn't always gotten along that well—back in junior high, they were infamous for the horrendous practical jokes they played on each other—but in the past couple of years they had both grown up a lot, and now they truly seemed to enjoy each other's company.

"Hey, don't look for any sympathy from me," Carole joked weakly. "Hanging out at Pine Hollow whenever you want still sounds pretty great to me, Alex or no Alex."

"I know." Stevie lowered her rake and gave Carole an understanding look. "Sorry, I didn't mean to complain. It really isn't the same without all you guys, but it's not like I'm totally without fun. Belle and I are bonding big-time, plus I've been helping Deborah with some research for an article she's writing about retired show horses. She even invited me to go on an interview with her tomorrow. We're going to ride up and talk to the old lady who runs the retirement farm."

"That sounds like fun," Carole commented,

pausing in her work just long enough to push back a stray curl that had escaped from her braid.

Stevie rolled her eyes. "Well, I don't know about *fun*, as in *yee-ha, whoopee*," she said. "But at least it will be a change of scenery."

"Yeah," Carole said glumly. "And at least there will be horses where you're going."

"True," Stevie admitted.

The two girls lapsed into silence once again as they moved down the path, still raking. Carole couldn't seem to stop thinking about the way life was going on at Pine Hollow without her. "So things are generally okay at the stable, then," she said at last. "Max and Red and the others aren't overwhelmed with work because I'm not there?"

Stevie shrugged. "I guess not," she said. "Although Denise was out sick for a couple of days, so naturally the others were all moaning and groaning about all the work there was to do." She shot Carole a sidelong glance. "But actually, that brings up some other news. I sort of accidentally overheard Max on the phone yesterday—"

"Sort of accidentally?" Carole smiled. Stevie was famous for her insatiable curiosity, and she wasn't above a little eavesdropping when it suited her.

Stevie shrugged again. "Hey, you know how close the tack room is to the office," she said. "But anyway, Max was talking to some friend of his at another stable, and he mentioned that he's started looking for a new stable hand."

Carole winced. She knew that Max planned to hire someone soon, though he'd told her it wouldn't really be a replacement. Her job would be waiting for her when the grounding was over. Still, she couldn't help feeling a little weird about Stevie's news. "That's good," she said carefully. "Max and the others work really hard. It will be good to have someone to help out."

Stevie looked up from her raking with a skeptical expression on her face. "Yeah, right," she said.

"No, I mean it," Carole said quickly. "They all put in a lot of hours—not just Max, but Red and Denise, too, and, well . . ."

"Ben," Stevie finished for her.

Carole blushed, thinking about her encounter with Ben the day before. She realized she still hadn't told Stevie or Lisa about that kiss. Glancing around, she decided this wasn't the time or place for that. But she had to at least talk to Stevie about his behavior the day before.

"Hey, speaking of Ben, guess who showed up here yesterday?" she said, trying to sound casual.

Judging by the sudden sharp interest in Stevie's eyes, Carole hadn't fooled her for a second. "Really?" Stevie said. "Did he come to see you?"

"Hardly." Carole could feel her face turning redder than ever. She quickly told Stevie about seeing Ben with the little girl, Zani, and then how he'd hurried away after seeing the volunteers in the park. When she finished, she shrugged. "I'm not sure if he spotted me or not. But it was totally weird either way."

Stevie rubbed her chin. "Wow," she said. "Sounds like maybe he did see you, and he didn't want you to catch him hanging out with the little girl. Who do you think she is, anyway?"

"I've been thinking about that a lot, actually," Carole admitted. "And I'm just not sure. At first I assumed she was his sister. But the thing is, she couldn't be more than three or four years old. And Ben's, like, almost twenty."

Stevie nodded thoughtfully. "That's a big gap in age," she commented. "Especially when there's no sign of a mother anywhere around." She shrugged. "Still, anything's possible. Maybe she's his half sister—you know, like Lisa and Lily. Same dad, younger mother. Or maybe their mom got pregnant late in life and died in childbirth or something."

Carole shook her head slowly. "I don't think so," she said. "Not about the second theory, anyway. One time Ben was talking about his family—"

"Really?" Stevie raised an eyebrow in surprise. "Are you sure? I didn't think he talked about anything that wasn't horse-related. Sort of like certain other people I could mention." She grinned to show that she was teasing.

Carole smiled, but her mind wasn't on Stevie's jokes. She was still thinking about Ben, trying to figure out how to reconcile the little she knew about Ben's past with what she'd seen the afternoon before. "No, but seriously," she told Stevie. "He said something once about his mother dying. I got the impression it happened a while ago—as in, longer ago than Zani's been around."

"Are you sure?"

Carole shook her head. She wasn't sure. As hard as she tried, she couldn't remember exactly what Ben had said to make her think that. But she couldn't shake the feeling that it was true, either. At the time, she remembered thinking that it was one more thing they had in common—both of them had lost their mothers too soon.

"I don't know," she said. "I just don't think the timing is quite right, that's all."

Stevie jabbed at a half-buried rock with her rake. "Okay, then," she said. "What about the half sister thing?"

Before Carole could answer, she saw Dr. Durbin approaching. "Well now, Carole," the vice principal said. "Who's your friend?" Her voice was pleasant enough, but Carole knew better than to try to fool her. Plenty of Willow Creek High students had tried and paid dearly for it. "This is my friend Stevie," Carole said. "She just stopped by to help out."

"Wonderful." Dr. Durbin smiled and clapped her hands briskly. "Then why don't you leave her to the raking and come with me, Carole? We could use your help over in the painting department."

Shooting Stevie a helpless, apologetic glance, Carole agreed.

*Yikes!* Lisa thought as she pulled a head of lettuce out of the refrigerator. *How did things get so weird around here so fast?*

She moved over to the butcher-block counter, stepping around Lily, who was playing on the floor with some blocks. As she grabbed the wooden salad bowl from the cabinet over the counter, Lisa sneaked a peek at Greta, who was sitting at the kitchen table peeling an apple. It was hard to believe that this total stranger was part of their family now. It was even weirder to think that her big brother was actually *married*. And had stepchildren.

"Greta, when you're finished with that, could you grab some salad dressing out of the fridge?" Evelyn asked from the stove, where she was making an omelet. "Then lunch should be just about ready."

Greta shrugged. "All right, if you say so," she

said. "But the men are still not yet returned from the golf course."

"I'm sure they'll be home soon," Lisa put in, breaking the lettuce apart into a large wooden bowl. "And Dad's always starved after a morning on the links. He'll be ready to eat right away."

"All right," Greta said again, in a tone that implied she had serious doubts about what Lisa had just said.

Lisa gritted her teeth, wondering if she was the only one who found her new sister-in-law a little hard to take sometimes. Greta certainly wasn't making much of an effort to fit in. That was making it even harder for Lisa to adjust to the idea that she was family, even though in some ways Lisa couldn't help thinking that she couldn't have asked for anyone better for her brother.

*I mean, get real,* Lisa told herself. *A glamorous European sister-in-law? And one that makes her living buying and selling horses? It should be a dream come true.*

And so far, Greta's sudden appearance *did* seem a little like a dream—one of those long, confusing ones where people kept shifting identities and nothing was quite the way it was supposed to be. Everyone was acting odd: Mr. Atwood kept clearing his throat and glaring at walls, Evelyn was acting so chipper and cheerful that she was like one of those sitcom moms from the 1950s, and Lisa herself wasn't sure what to say or do from one moment to the next. And of course, Greta was the strangest one of all, since none of them knew what to expect from her. And it wasn't as if she was making much of an effort to get acquainted. In fact, she had spent most of the previous evening on the phone, talking in German to clients and to her family in Germany. Then, that morning, she had announced at breakfast that she needed Peter to take her shopping. They had returned just in time for Peter to head off to the golf course with his father.

"Here we go, the apples are ready," Greta announced, dumping the fruit she'd just finished peeling and cutting onto a platter that Evelyn had set on the table. "Now I will get the salad dressing." She stood, smoothing her ivory slacks, and headed for the refrigerator.

"You speak English so well, Greta," Lisa commented politely, deciding it was time to start making more of an effort herself. "Did you study it in school?"

Greta shrugged. "It is not a difficult language to master when one speaks German," she replied offhandedly. "Besides, I am very interested in languages—it is one of the things my Peter and I have in common."

Trying not to grimace at her use of *my Peter,* Lisa opened her mouth to respond. But just then there was a loud shriek from right outside the kitchen, and a second later Greta's two children—Lisa still couldn't think of them as in any way belonging to Peter—raced into the room.

The older one, Dieter, was about seven years old, with longish wheat-colored hair and a turned-up nose. Hanni, his sister, was a couple of years younger. She wore her brown hair in shoulder-length pigtails, and her eyes were just as blue and direct as her mother's.

"Mama!" Dieter cried breathlessly. "Hanni, she is being a big jerk! Tell her to stop right now!"

"*Nein, nein,* Mama!" Hanni cried. Then she launched into a torrent of German mixed with French and a little English, which Lisa found completely impossible to follow.

Greta dropped the salad dressing on the counter and hurried over to her children, clucking soothingly to them. Speaking softly in German, she managed to calm them and shoo them out of the room.

"They're lively kids," Evelyn said cheerfully as she slid an omelet onto a plate.

"Yes, they are marvelous." Greta gazed fondly in the direction the children had gone. "I do not know what I would do without them. It was my one great concern when I—ah, what is the word *auf englisch?*—divorced from their father a year ago."

Lisa couldn't help raising her eyebrows at that. "A year?" she said. "You've only been divorced for a year? Then how long have you been going out with Peter?"

Greta smiled, a faraway look coming into her eyes. "My Peter—I do not remember life before him. It has been two wonderful months."

"Two months?" Lisa repeated in disbelief.

"Yes, that is right—two. *Zwei*." Greta held up two fingers. "Two."

"Let me get this straight," Lisa said. "You've only known each other for two months, and you decided to get married?"

Evelyn shot Lisa a worried glance from the stove. "Sometimes love is like that," she said lightly. "It happens fast. After all, Lisa, your father and I had only known each other a few months when we started talking about marriage."

Lisa clenched her fists, suddenly wishing that Evelyn would just go away for a while. *You know, she's starting to sound an awful lot like Mom,* she thought, shooting her stepmother a quick, annoyed glance. *Always trying to make nice, keep everyone polite and happy—at least on the surface—no matter what else is happening.*

Before anyone could say anything else, Greta's kids raced back in. This time they didn't seem to be angry with each other. Both were laughing and jumping up and down with excitement.

"Mama, we're hungry," Hanni announced. "When will we eat?"

"I hope it's soon." Dieter glanced at Lisa and Evelyn and then rattled off a question in French. Even though she'd taken the language for several years in school, Lisa couldn't follow what the boy was saying.

She waited, expecting Greta to translate for them or at least respond in English so that they could figure it out. Instead, Greta let out a loud laugh and then replied in rapid-fire German.

Lisa grimaced. *Nice manners,* she thought, feeling a little like her mother now herself but not really caring. *We all know Greta and those kids can speak English as well as the rest of us. So why can't they stick to it when the rest of us are around?*

Deciding it was time to switch to a safer subject, Lisa took a deep breath and then forced herself to smile at Greta as the children ran out of the room once again, almost tripping over Lily on their way. "So, Greta," Lisa said. "It must be really interesting to travel all over the world looking at horses."

"Oh, yes, it is interesting," Greta replied. "Do not think my job is easy, though. It is not like going to one of your malls and shopping."

"Of course not," Lisa said politely. "I'm a rider myself, as Peter must have told you, and so I realize—"

"Ah, yes, that is right," Greta interrupted. "Peter did say something of the sort. He said you and your friends, you go trail riding often."

"Well, yes, but that's not all we do." Lisa wondered why just a few words from Greta made her feel so defensive. "I mean, I've been taking lessons since junior high, and I've been in lots of shows and stuff, too. I've done tons of jumping, and competed in dressage and equitation, and even done some other kinds of things like foxhunting and polocrosse."

"Yes, Lisa is quite the equestrienne," Evelyn broke in cheerily. "But why don't you tell us more about your work, Greta?"

"Of course." Greta smiled, then started chattering about all the top-notch horses she'd found for riders all over Europe.

Lisa hardly paid attention. She was too busy trying to calm herself down and convince herself that Greta hadn't meant any harm by her comments. *She probably runs into people who think they're horse experts all the time,* she thought. *And if all Peter told her about my riding is that his little sister likes to go on trail rides with her friends, it's no wonder if Greta assumed I was just a casual weekend rider.* She glanced at her sister-in-law with a slight frown. *Still, we're supposed to be family now. Couldn't she at least give me the benefit of the doubt?*

"Hello! Anyone home?" Peter called, stepping through the back door.

Lisa turned to look at him. Her brother's words had been light and casual, but the deep crease in his forehead made her suspect that his golf game with his father hadn't exactly been relaxing. When Mr. Atwood stepped into the kitchen behind him, his tense expression removed any remaining doubt.

Lisa winced. *I totally feel for him,* she thought as Peter stepped over to give Greta a kiss and Mr. Atwood dumped his golf bag in the corner near the door. *After all, I definitely know what it's like to do something our parents disapprove of—and hear about it, over and over and over again, until you just want to scream.*

Evelyn stepped over to greet her husband with a kiss and her stepson with a pat on the arm. "So," she said pleasantly. "How was the golf game?"

Lisa rolled her eyes. Evelyn couldn't possibly be dense enough not to notice the tension between father and son. That meant she had decided to ignore it.

"Fine," Peter said tersely. "Nice course."

"That's good," Evelyn chirped. "Then you must be hungry. Lunch is just about ready."

As Evelyn hurried to fetch the omelets and bring them to the table, and as Greta stepped into the hall to call Dieter and Hanni, Lisa took her place beside Peter. "You okay?" she whispered to him when she was pretty sure no one else was listening.

He shrugged, not meeting her eye. "Been bet-

**101**

ter," he muttered. "Dad just doesn't know when to let up sometimes, you know?"

"I know." Lisa grimaced, glancing over at her father, who was lowering Lily into her high chair. "Believe me, I know."

Soon everyone was settled around the table, helping themselves to salad and omelets and juice. For a minute or two, the conversation centered around the men's golf game and the amenities of the local golf club.

"You should really come along and check it out next time, *Liebchen*," Peter commented, reaching over to squeeze Greta's hand. "They have a nice pool, a restaurant, and some tennis courts."

"Ah, yes?" Greta looked interested. "I would like to see the courts. I used to play tennis quite a lot as a teen. My sister and I, we won our regional tournament in doubles two years in a row."

Peter smiled at her. "Is that right? I didn't even know you played tennis," he said.

Mr. Atwood cleared his throat. "After only two months of acquaintance, there's quite a bit you two don't know about each other, I'll wager."

Greta pursed her lips but kept quiet. Lisa felt her own cheeks turning pink. Did her father really have to be so negative about anything new and different? The rest of the table was silent. Even Dieter and Hanni were staring at Mr. Atwood with wide, surprised eyes. Only baby Lily seemed unaffected as she played with a piece of lettuce in her bowl.

After a quick glance at his new wife, Peter turned to glare at his father. "Look, Dad. Enough is enough. Can't we just have a nice family lunch and talk about something else?" he said.

"Exactly what I was thinking," Evelyn put in quickly.

Mr. Atwood hardly seemed to hear his wife's remark. He glared at Peter. "Of course, son," he said. "Why discuss anything important? After all, we're only your family, that's all." With a scowl, he returned his attention to his plate. "We're just lucky your mother isn't here right now," he muttered under his breath, but loudly enough for everyone at the table to hear.

Lisa winced. Peter had left their mother a message the night before, saying that he was in L.A. and that he had a big surprise to share with her. Knowing their mother, Lisa was sure she would be on the phone to California the second she heard that message, no matter what time of day it was in either place. The fact that she hadn't called yet, nearly eighteen hours later, was a sure sign that she was off somewhere with Rafe.

*Bleagh,* Lisa thought. *As if I don't have enough on my mind right now with everything else that's going on—now I also have that disgusting image in my mind!*

She pushed that aside for the moment. "Dad," she said, "I really don't think you're being fair to Peter and Greta. It's their life, and if they love each other, why shouldn't they get married? It makes perfect sense to me."

Her father glared at her over his fork. "I hardly think you're the one who should be lecturing us all on rational behavior, Lisa," he said coolly.

"Whatever," Lisa replied, feeling a little hurt but plowing on regardless. After all, what better way to start forging a friendship with Greta than to show her that she was on her side? "I just think you should give them a chance, that's all."

Lisa glanced at Greta, but the woman hardly seemed to be paying attention to the conversation. She was cutting up the lettuce in Dieter's salad into tiny pieces. Lisa sighed. So much for her show of sisterly solidarity.

"Peter, darling." Greta spoke up suddenly, glancing up from her son's plate. "We have not discussed our plans for the horse show on Wednesday. Are you going to be able to come along to watch the children? I will be working, and cannot be with them at every moment."

"Sure," Peter said. "Count me in." He glanced around the table. "Actually, maybe we should all go together. As a family. I think maybe we all just need to spend a little more time together—you know, getting acquainted."

Lisa almost smiled at the look of dismay that crossed Greta's face at that. "Sure," Lisa said casually, unable to resist. "Count me in, too. Sounds like fun."

Peter nodded, shooting Lisa a smile. Then Greta put a hand on his arm and said something rather lengthy in German. Peter nodded along with her words, not even seeming to notice that his wife was speaking a language that no one else at the table could understand. And once again, Lisa couldn't help noting that Greta didn't seem to realize or care how rude she was being to her new family.

*New family.* The thought brought Lisa up short. *That's what we are now,* she thought. *Her family. She's our family.*

It wasn't the first time she'd thought it in the past twenty-four hours, but it was the first time its full meaning had really sunk in. Lisa glanced over at Greta, who had returned to her task of cutting up Dieter's salad; at Mr. Atwood, who was staring into space and chewing slowly, a distraught expression on his face; and then at Peter, who was leaning over to help Hanni pour herself more juice.

Lisa bit her lip. *That means we're all stuck with each other, like it or not. So maybe we all need to try a little harder to make the best of it.*

# SEVEN

Stevie was in a good mood as she strode through the big double doors of Pine Hollow on Tuesday morning. The weather was just about as good as it ever got in November—crisp, cool, and sunny. For a moment, she considered backing out of her plans to accompany Deborah for her story to take advantage of the perfect trail-riding weather.

Then she thought better of it. *What fun is it to go on a trail ride all by yourself?* she thought with a slight frown. Not only were her usual riding partners all still absent for their various reasons, but even Alex had been nowhere to be found when she'd left home a few minutes earlier. She guessed that meant he had finally wearied of moping around the stable missing Lisa and decided to hang out with his other friends or something. *Anyway,* Stevie thought with a sigh, *I promised Deborah I'd go with her. And even if having tea and chatting with some little old lady doesn't exactly qualify as covering breaking news, it's always pretty interesting to watch Deborah at work.*

As usual, Stevie turned first toward Belle's stall, planning to check on the mare quickly before going to meet Deborah. When she arrived at the stall and peered over the half door, the mare was lying on the thick layer of bedding on the stall floor. She heaved herself to her feet with a snort as soon as Stevie unlatched the door.

"Hey, toots," Stevie greeted her horse fondly, making a move to sling one arm around her neck.

Just in time, she spotted a large manure stain on Belle's withers. Stopping her arm in midair and glancing at the floor, Stevie immediately spotted the culprit—a large pile of squashed manure. Obviously, Belle had lain down on it as she rested, probably not even noticing it was there.

"Yuck," Stevie said, wrinkling her nose and settling for scratching Belle's neck. "I think maybe this calls for a little quick grooming before I leave." Glancing at her watch, she saw that she still had a few minutes before she was supposed to meet Deborah up at her house. "Be back in a jiff, girl," she told Belle with a pat. Then she let herself out of the stall and headed down the aisle toward the tack room.

She was so busy mentally reviewing how long it would take her to retrieve her grooming kit, return to the stall, and get Belle cleaned up that she was halfway into the room before she recognized its other occupant. Nicole Adams was perched on a tack trunk, wearing skintight ivory breeches and a wool ski sweater and carefully polishing one of her mahogany-colored leather riding boots with a soft rag.

*Yikes!* Stevie thought, skidding to a stop. *What's she doing here again?*

Nicole didn't keep her in suspense for long. "Hi, Stevie," she said. "Did Alex ride over with you? We're supposed to meet up in a little while—he thought it was a perfect day for a nice ride through the woods."

"Um, no," Stevie said, taken completely by surprise. If Alex was coming to Pine Hollow today, why hadn't he mentioned it at breakfast? He knew Stevie was driving over. "Uh, I haven't seem him lately."

"Oh, okay." Nicole shrugged and returned to her task, seeming unperturbed. "Well, I'm sure he'll be here soon."

"I'm sure," Stevie said shortly. This was getting ridiculous. Clueless or not, Alex had to shape up and realize what was happening. Stevie was positive that Nicole had only started coming to Pine Hollow as an excuse to leech on to Alex. And Alex seemed to be letting it happen without a single protest.

*I know how Nicole works,* Stevie thought grimly,

taking a couple of steps farther into the room. *She must've liked flirting with Alex at that party at our house while he and Lisa were broken up, so she decided to totally ignore the fact that they got back together right after the party. She probably borrowed those boots and breeches from Veronica.*

Veronica diAngelo had been one of Stevie's least favorite people when she'd ridden regularly at Pine Hollow, and that hadn't changed much. Veronica and Nicole were part of the same clique at Fenton Hall, and Stevie was sure Veronica would like nothing better than to mess up Stevie's and Alex's lives. Veronica wasn't too crazy about Lisa, either, so Stevie was sure that trying to destroy her relationship would definitely be a bonus in Veronica's eyes.

*But she won't be able to do it,* Stevie vowed, clenching her fists. *Not if I have anything to say about it.*

It was time to talk to Nicole. Taking a deep breath, Stevie decided to plunge right in. "Listen, Nicole," she said. "There's something I've been wanting to say to you for a couple of days now."

"What is it, Stevie?" Nicole asked, barely glancing up from her boot as she rubbed at a tiny dull spot on the heel.

"It's about Alex." Stevie paused to see what Nicole's reaction would be.

Nicole just shrugged. "What about him?"

*Okay, so she's not going to make this easy,* Stevie thought. *Fine. If she wants to play dumb, I'll play along.*

"I've noticed that you and Alex have been spending a lot of time together over the past few days," she said, speaking slowly and distinctly, "and I just wanted to remind you that he has a girlfriend. A *serious* girlfriend. Who just happens to be my best friend. And I'd hate to see anyone get in the way of all that, if you know what I mean."

"No." Nicole crossed her arms over her chest and blinked at Stevie. "As a matter of fact, I'm really not sure what you're talking about. What does any of this have to do with me? Alex and I are just hanging out, that's all. Having a little fun. I mean, we're just two friends who both happen to like going riding once in a while. What's wrong with that?"

"I'll tell you what's wrong with that," Stevie snapped, feeling her last shred of patience spiraling rapidly away. "What's wrong is that Alex only started riding because he knows how important it is to Lisa. And get real—it's not like you've ever shown any interest in—"

"Nicole!" a hearty voice interrupted Stevie's rant. "There you are!"

"Hi, Max," Nicole cooed, standing up as the stable owner strode into the tack room, his delighted smile stretching from ear to ear. "I was wondering if I was ever going to run into you."

As Nicole took a step toward Max, he hurried right up to her and gave her a quick hug. "I don't know," he said, stepping back. "You've grown up so much since I saw you last, I wouldn't have recognized you. How many years has it been?"

"Too many," Nicole replied with a giggle.

Stevie just goggled in dumbfounded amazement. *Huh?* she thought. *Max and Nicole are acting like they're old friends or long-lost relatives or something. What's up with that?*

Max finally seemed to notice Stevie standing there staring at him. "Oh, hello, Stevie," he said. "I think Deb's waiting for you up at the house."

"Uh—yeah," Stevie said. She was still searching her mind for an explanation for this inexplicable scene. "I know. I was just on my way, but . . . So what's going on? Do you and Nicole, like, know each other? How? Is it through Veronica?"

"Veronica?" Max wrinkled his brow. "What are you talking about? Nicole used to ride here, remember?"

Stevie put one hand to her head, wondering if this could possibly be some kind of truly bizarre dream. "She used to ride here? In what universe?" she cried. "She never rode here! Not until, like, three days ago."

Max looked confused, but Nicole just giggled

**111**

again. "I think I stopped riding just before Stevie started taking lessons, Max," she explained. "That's why she doesn't remember."

"Ah." Max looked satisfied with that. "Yes, that's right." He shook his head. "I'll tell you, Stevie, it was a sad day at Pine Hollow when Nicole came and told me she was quitting riding so that she could take gymnastics. I remember it like it was yesterday. She was only about eight years old at the time, but she had a better seat than most of the intermediate class."

Nicole's cheeks flushed pink. "Oh, come on, Max," she said. "I wasn't that good."

"You were," Max insisted. "You had perfect balance, a real feel for a horse—basically, more natural talent than I'd seen in a long time. And trust me, I don't make comments like that lightly."

"That's for sure," Stevie muttered, remembering all the times over the years when Max had criticized her posture or yelled at her to stop riding like a sack of potatoes. And as far as she could recall, he'd never once gushed over her "natural talent."

"Well, I finally decided I'd been away long enough," Nicole said. "I just hope I'm not too rusty after all these years."

"I'm sure you'll be fine." Max was still grinning. "Which horse have you been riding so far?"

"Well, that stable hand—what's his name?

112

O'Malley?" Nicole shrugged. "He suggested I try out this big bay named Congo."

"Hmmm. He's a nice horse, but really more for beginners." Max waved one hand. "You could handle a much more spirited horse—maybe Topside. I think you'd really like him. He used to be a show horse, and he's still got a lot of spirit. If Red has any doubts, just tell him to come and talk to me. I'll make sure he knows you're more than capable of handling him." He chuckled. "If I have to, I'll even tell him the story of your first ride on Comanche. Do you remember how he took off across the big west field and . . . ?"

*Ugh*, Stevie thought. *If Max keeps babbling about how great Nicole is, I just might have to hurl.*

Max's lavish praise wasn't the only thing that was making Stevie feel a little sick, though. She was starting to realize that she might have been wrong about Nicole's motives. And she didn't like being wrong. Still, now that she had a little more information, she had to admit that it was possible Nicole might not be hanging around the stable for the sole purpose of sinking her claws into Alex. Maybe Stevie was just being paranoid on Lisa's behalf because of all the trouble she and Alex had been having lately. In fact, now that Stevie stopped to think about it, she did have some vague memories of overhearing Nicole and Veronica chatting about riding once or twice over the years. She hadn't thought much about it at the time, but now . . .

At that moment, Max interrupted his monologue about Nicole's first horse show to glance over. "Stevie," he said sharply. "Are you still here? I thought you were leaving to meet my wife."

"Oh, yeah," Stevie muttered, jolted out of her thoughts. Whatever was going on with Nicole and Alex, she didn't have time to worry about it now. *In fact, maybe I shouldn't worry about it at all,* she told herself, smiling weakly at Nicole and Max as she backed out of the room. *Maybe I should just ignore it. After all, Lisa will be back in a few days. And that will be that.*

Checking her watch, Stevie saw that she was officially late to meet Deborah. With a mental apology to Belle, she hurried out of the tack room and broke into a jog as she headed for the back exit.

Lisa glanced up and down the upstairs hall as she grabbed the cordless phone off the table near the stairs and scooted into her room at the end of the hall. She was feeling in desperate need of moral support, and she didn't want anyone in her family to overhear her calling her friends.

Closing the door softly behind her, Lisa briefly surveyed the small bedroom, which her father had designated as Lisa's when he and Evelyn had bought the house. Lisa had helped decorate it on one of her first visits to California, and she had taken the opportunity to try something a little different. Instead of the muted, feminine florals and tasteful white wicker that filled her bedroom in Virginia, she had chosen a black-and-white-patterned fabric for the curtains, a shaggy white rug for the bleached pine floor, and a bold turquoise for the walls. It was very different from any style she'd ever considered before, and she felt almost as comfortable in the room as she did in her bedroom back home.

Today, though, as she crossed the floor to her platform bed, she wasn't really seeing the room in front of her. Instead, her mind was flashing back over the past two days. Despite her vow to try harder to get to know Greta better, Lisa wasn't finding it any easier to get along with her sister-in-law.

*It's weird,* she thought. *It's as if Greta doesn't even care about us being friends, let alone sisters. Am I the only one who's noticed that around here?* Flopping onto the black-and-white-striped bedspread, Lisa quickly dialed the Lakes' number.

"Come on, come on," she muttered as she punched in the last number. "Be there!" Glancing at her watch, she realized that her chances were pretty slim. It was just after eleven o'clock in California, which meant it was around two P.M. in

Virginia. No doubt Stevie and Alex were out some-where, enjoying their newfound freedom at the stable or the mall or the basketball courts at the park.

After a moment of silence as the call went through, the impatient buzz of a busy signal met Lisa's ear. With a sigh, she hit the button to hang up. *What now?* she wondered. She could try again in a few minutes, of course, but Evelyn had said something about trying to dash out and get her hair done, so Lisa was expecting her stepmother to track her down for baby-sitting duty at any mo-ment. She wished she could call Carole, but she knew better than to try. Colonel Hanson had been very clear that his daughter wasn't allowed to chat on the phone while she was grounded, and the last thing Lisa wanted to do was get her friend into even more trouble.

Feeling impatient, she punched in the Lakes' number again. This time the phone rang once on the other end; then someone picked up.

"Hello?" a breathless voice greeted her. "Fawn?"

"Michael?" Lisa smiled. Stevie's thirteen-year-old brother had recently started dating a girl in his class. It was his first real romance, and Lisa couldn't help feeling a little amazed every time she thought about it. Somehow she still thought of Michael as the rambunctious nine-year-old he had been when she'd first become friends with Stevie. "Hi, it's Lisa. Is Stevie or Alex there?"

"Lisa?" Michael sounded perplexed. "I thought you were in California."

"I am," Lisa said teasingly. "They have phones here, too, you know."

Michael snorted, his usual response to any joke made by anyone over the age of fifteen. "Whatever," he said. "Anyway, Stevie and Alex are out. They're both over at the stable, I think."

"Really?" Lisa wasn't the least bit surprised to learn that Stevie was at Pine Hollow. But Alex? He didn't usually go to the stable without her.

*Still, I guess maybe I shouldn't be surprised by that, either,* Lisa thought with a smile. *After being grounded for so long, even hanging out at Pine Hollow with his sister probably seems like a big treat to Alex.*

"Okay," she told Michael. "Well, could you let them know I called? No particular message or anything—just wanted to say hi."

"Yeah, okay," Michael said.

"Bye," Lisa said. "Happy Thanksg—"

"Hello?" a new voice broke onto the line with a click. "Is someone on the line, please? I am wanting to make a call."

"Greta?" Lisa said, startled by the interruption.

"Yes, it is I," Greta replied. "Who is this, please?"

"It's me. Lisa." Lisa grimaced. Did her sister-in-law always have to sound so imperious about everything? "I'm just finishing up a call myself. I'll only be a moment."

"Uh, right," Michael broke in, sounding confused. "Well, bye, Lisa."

"Bye." Lisa took a deep breath as Michael hung up, trying to keep control of her temper.

"Are you finished now?" Greta asked impatiently. "It is very important that I place my call soon."

"Yeah, I'm sure it is," Lisa snapped, fed up with Greta's attitude. "*Pardon me* for using the phone in my own dad's house." She punched the off button before Greta could respond.

She felt a little guilty about snapping at her sister-in-law. *Still, she asked for it,* she told herself defensively as she wandered across the room and out into the hall. She scowled, remembering some of her exchanges with Greta over the past couple of days. *She's always acting like everything she has to do is so much more important than anything anyone else is doing. And like she knows just everything there is to know about things, like horses for instance. . . .*

Starting down the stairs, Lisa heard loud voices coming from two directions at once. To her left, she could hear Greta speaking rapidly in German—apparently she was on the phone in the kitchen. Judging by the voice coming from the direction of the living room, her father was busy lecturing Peter once again on impulsive choices and the heartache they invariably caused.

*Yow*, Lisa thought, wincing on her brother's behalf as her father said something about planning for the future and being rational. *Dad's really going after him now that Greta's out of the room. What does he think that's going to accomplish, anyway? Talk about not being rational! I mean, they're already married. You'd think he could be at least a teeny bit supportive of that.*

Her heart went out to her brother. She knew exactly how he felt. He'd made his decision, he was living his life, and she was sure he didn't appreciate having his father second-guess his choices.

*Well, I'm not going to do that to him*, Lisa told herself, feeling another flash of guilt about her hasty words to Greta a few minutes earlier. *I might not be crazy about Greta right now, but that doesn't mean I can't support Peter's decision marry her.* She rolled her eyes as her father made a loud comment about actions and consequences. *And it sounds like I might be the only one who is supporting him right about now.*

She strode into the living room, planning to join in the discussion and show her brother that he wasn't totally alone. She found her father and brother glaring at each other from opposite ends of the room. Peter was pacing in front of the small blue-tiled fireplace; Mr. Atwood was perched on the edge of the overstuffed sofa. Evelyn was sitting beside her husband, her hands clenched tightly in her lap, looking as though she wished she could sink into the cushions and disappear. Before Lisa could say a word to any of them, Peter looked over and saw her.

"Lisa!" he cried, hurrying toward her. "There you are. Listen, I was talking to Greta just now—she needs to go check out a couple of horses this afternoon at a farm near here. I thought I'd ride over there with her—you know, keep her company. What do you say? Want to come with us?"

Lisa hesitated for a second. She could still hear Greta chattering away loudly on the phone in the other room. Did she really want to spend the whole afternoon with her?

Still, when she looked from her brother's hopeful smile to her father's disapproving frown, she knew what she had to say. "Sure," she replied, trying to sound casual. "That sounds like fun."

"Great!" Peter looked relieved. He turned to Evelyn. "Hey, do you think you could keep an eye on the kids for us? They're having so much fun here, I'd hate to drag them away now."

Lisa had almost forgotten about Greta's kids. Glancing out the living room window, she saw that Dieter and Hanni were chasing each other around the small, neat backyard. Nearby, Lily was

120

swinging contentedly in her automated baby swing as she watched the older kids play.

Evelyn glanced at Mr. Atwood with a slight frown. "All right," she said after a second. "I suppose I could do that. I can reschedule my hair appointment."

"Thanks." Peter didn't seem to notice his stepmother's slightly disgruntled expression. He clapped his hands together and smiled at Lisa. "That will give the three of us plenty of time to chat."

"Great." Lisa smiled weakly. She guessed Peter was hoping she and Greta would have a chance to bond over their common interest in horses.

*Of course, he's also probably just hoping to escape for a while himself,* she added, shooting a quick look at her father and stepmother. Her father was leaning back on the sofa, his arms crossed over his chest and a grumpy expression on his face. Evelyn was tugging distractedly at a lock of her short blond hair as she stared out the back window at the kids in the yard. *And who can blame him for that?*

At that moment, the loud torrent of German from the other room suddenly stopped. A few seconds later Greta hurried into the room, a strange expression on her face.

"Peter," she said. "There is a call for you on the second line. I have ended my call."

"Oh, you didn't have to do that, darling," Peter said with a smile. "But who is it?"

Greta said something in German. Peter's smile quickly faded, and his face went pale.

"What is it?" Lisa asked. "Who's on the phone?"

Peter gulped nervously, hardly glancing at her as he hurried toward the kitchen. "It's Mom."

# EIGHT

"I think this is it." Stevie pointed to a gravel driveway leading to the right off the quiet country highway. She glanced at the handwritten directions Deborah had given her to follow. "Number twenty-seven. Yep."

"Okay." Deborah spun the wheel of her blue hatchback and pulled up the drive to a small parking area beside a white frame farmhouse. "Here we are. Let's get this over with."

Stevie shot her a bemused look. "Nice attitude, Ms. Dedicated Reporter," she said. "Where's your sense of adventure? For all we know, this could be the article that wins you the Pulitzer Prize."

"Yeah, right." Deborah rolled her eyes, but she also cracked a smile.

The two of them climbed out of the car. As Deborah fetched her pad and tape recorder from the backseat, Stevie stretched and took a look around. Several horses were grazing in a good-sized pasture to one side of the house. Nearby was a large old barn. The green paint was peeling off its sides, but otherwise it appeared to be in good repair.

"Nice place," Stevie commented. "I wouldn't mind retiring here myself."

Deborah chuckled. "Hey, wait a minute. You aren't allowed to start talking about retiring until you actually have a job."

"You think being in high school isn't a job?" Stevie joked. She waited while Deborah closed the car door; then the two of them headed for the uneven brick walk leading to the front porch.

Before they could reach the door, it swung open, revealing a stout, grandmotherly woman with gray hair pulled back in a messy bun. Her broad, apple-checked face wore a cheerful smile, and her small, light blue eyes twinkled with pleasure.

"Welcome!" the woman cried heartily, wiping her plump hands on the gingham apron that was tied over her khaki slacks and white blouse. "You must be the reporters. Hello! I'm Mrs. Monroe."

"Hello," Deborah replied. "I'm Deborah Hale. This is Stevie Lake, my intern."

Stevie smiled and gave a little wave. *Wow*, she thought. *Check out Grandma Moses. Did she just step out of central casting or what? She's such a cliché it's almost scary.*

She instantly felt a little guilty for the uncharitable thought, especially when Mrs. Monroe invited them inside for tea and homemade cookies. After all, what was wrong with being a perfect grandma type?

Mrs. Monroe shooed the two visitors into the front parlor, which was furnished with dusty antiques and lots of brocade. Stevie glanced around. "Nice house," she said politely.

"Oh, thank you, dear!" Mrs. Monroe exclaimed, rushing over and patting Stevie on the shoulder. "It's so nice of you to say so! Now, just sit down and make yourselves comfy. I'll be back in a jiff with our refreshments."

As the woman bustled off toward the back of the house, Stevie looked at Deborah, who was taking a seat on the edge of a red velvet Victorian sofa. "Wow," she said, keeping her voice low so that their hostess wouldn't hear. "Quite a place, huh?"

"I'm sorry I made you come along, Stevie," Deborah returned in the same low tone. "I don't think this is going to be a very interesting interview. I'll try to keep it as short as possible, okay?"

"You didn't make me come," Stevie insisted. "I wanted to come. And don't worry—I'm sure the interview will go fine. You're a star reporter, remember? You can make anything seem interesting."

Deborah smiled weakly at the compliment, but

before she could say anything more, Mrs. Monroe returned bearing an ornate silver tray laden with treats. After a flurry of activity—pouring tea, passing the sugar and cream, insisting that the guests help themselves to homemade cookies and lemon squares—Mrs. Monroe sat back in a creaky upholstered armchair with a contented sigh. "Now then," she said. "Shall we get acquainted?"

"Er, of course." Deborah glanced at the notepad on her lap. "Um, let's see. How did you first become involved with these retirees?"

"Oh, I just love all horses," the woman gushed. "I suppose it all started way back when I was a girl in Tennessee. You see, my grandfather had a small farm, and I loved spending time there. Oh, I spent many happy hours just lying on the grass beneath the apple trees, reading or whispering secrets to my older sister, Mabel. . . ."

*What does any of this have to do with horses?* Stevie wondered as Mrs. Monroe went on and on about life on the farm and then swerved off into a long, involved tale of the time her grandfather's tabby barn cat had nine kittens in the middle of a thunderstorm. The answer to Stevie's question didn't become apparent for a good five minutes, when the woman finally mentioned that her grandfather had bought the two sisters a pony.

"Mabel soon became more interested in going to dances and parties with boys than in visiting the farm and riding Breezy with me. But that dear old pony was my faithful companion for many a year." Mrs. Monroe let out a nostalgic sigh, clasping her hands in front of her. "I still miss the old rascal."

Stevie sneaked a glance at her watch. *I can't believe we've only been sitting here for twenty minutes,* she thought. *It feels more like twenty years.*

"Hmmm, I see." Deborah was looking a bit desperate as she checked her notes again. "Er, but perhaps we should talk about the horses you have staying here now."

"I have an even better idea," Stevie broke in. Despite her earlier assurances to Deborah, she was starting to feel as though she would go crazy if she had to sit in that dusty, dim room for one more minute. "Why don't we head out to the barn and take a look at the horses while we talk?"

Deborah looked relieved. "That's a great idea, Stevie," she said. She started to rise from her seat, glancing at Mrs. Monroe. "Shall we?"

Mrs. Monroe looked startled at the suggestion. "Oh, I don't know, girls," she said uncertainly. "Do you really want to go out there? It's much more comfortable in here, and there's plenty of tea left. . . ." She waved one plump hand at the teapot on the coffee table.

"Oh, but my story is really about the horses," Deborah said politely. "I do think I ought to take at least a quick look at them, don't you?" She gave the older woman a winning smile and held up her notebook. "Please, couldn't we see them, if it's not too much trouble?"

"Well, all right then." Mrs. Monroe set her teacup back on the tray and got to her feet. "Out we go."

Stevie swallowed a sigh of relief. Shooting a look at Deborah, she saw that the reporter looked just as happy as she was to be escaping from the stuffy sitting room.

*Okay, this is the last time I assume an investigative reporter's life is all adventure and excitement,* she thought as she followed the two women back into the hall. *Because compared to this interview, even school seems exciting!*


As she carefully dug rocks and pieces of broken glass and scraps of metal out of the small open center of the park, Carole found her gaze wandering frequently to the street to the west. So far there was no sign of Zani or any of her young friends, or of the old man the kids had called Gramps.

Or of Ben.

*Why did he have to kiss me in the first place?* Carole wondered, feeling the now familiar wave of confusion, anger, and embarrassment wash over her as she remembered that brief, unforgettable moment in the thicket at the showgrounds. *Why did he have to mess up everything between us?*

She bit her lip as she jabbed her small hand spade into the ground in front of her. Maybe she was the one who was to blame. After all, she couldn't quite recall exactly whose face had started moving closer, or whose lips had brushed the other's first. . . .

Feeling her face flush as she thought about it, Carole tossed a chunk of stone into the bucket at her side and frowned. *Why does my life have to be so complicated, anyway?* she wondered. *I mean, my friends don't have these problems. Stevie meets Phil at horse camp, and bam! it's love at first sight, and they stay together forever. Lisa and Alex trade a special glance across the dinner table one night, and bam! they're totally gaga and start finishing each other's sentences. Why can't it just happen that way for me? Why am I the one who somehow ends up kissing a guy who turns around the very same afternoon and acts like he's never even met me?*

Before she could figure out any answers to that, she heard someone calling her name. She didn't recognize the voice at first, but when she glanced over her shoulder, she saw Lionel, the friendly, earnest young man with the glasses, and his wife—what was her name again? Nadine?—walking toward her, hand in hand.

"Uh, hi," Carole said, wondering what they wanted. She wasn't exactly in the mood for small talk with her fellow volunteers. "What's up?"

Nadine shrugged and smiled. "We just finished watering the new shrubs, so we thought we'd come see if you needed any help over here."

Carole forced a smile in return. "Thanks," she said. "Um, but I think I've got it covered."

Lionel surveyed Carole's little patch of ground. "You're doing great, Carole," he said. "But we'll get it done a lot faster if the three of us work together. What do you say?"

What *could* she say? "Okay," Carole replied weakly. "Thanks."

Lionel and Nadine knelt and set to work on either side of Carole, chatting about the progress they were making at the park. Carole did her best to nod in all the right spots, but she was only half listening. The other half of her mind was still occupied with her own life. At the moment, it seemed to be in as much disarray as the park had been when they'd first arrived on Saturday.

After a few minutes, Carole suddenly noticed that Lionel was gazing at her, and she realized that he must have asked her a question she hadn't even heard. She gulped.

"Carole?" Nadine blinked at her, her round eyes concerned. "Are you all right?"

"Um, s-sorry," Carole stammered. "I guess I was kind of distracted there for a second. Uh, actually the stuff you were just saying reminded me of those kids who were hanging around here yesterday. Have you seen them today?"

"No," Nadine said softly. "But I noticed them yesterday, too." She traded an unreadable look with her husband.

Carole wasn't sure what that was all about. She felt a little uncomfortable as Nadine and Lionel continued to gaze at each other for a long, silent moment.

Suddenly noticing that Carole was watching them, Lionel smiled wanly. "Sorry. Guess we're the ones who are distracted now. It's just that talking or thinking about kids—well, it's kind of a sensitive subject for us, I guess."

"That's right," Nadine said softly. "You see, when Lionel and I got married, we both wanted a big family. I'd always dreamed about having six kids—"

"Until I convinced her we should try for ten," Lionel joked halfheartedly. He shrugged, glancing down at the rusty metal can he'd just dug out of the dirt. "Anyway, we figured we should get started right away. So when Nadine found out she was pregnant just a few months after our wedding, we were both thrilled. We called everyone we

131

knew, we bought out the local toy store, the works."

Carole couldn't help feeling a little impatient. She really wasn't in the mood for hearing her co-volunteers' life story. The next thing she knew, they would probably start pulling out baby pictures and kindergarten scribbles to show her.

But Nadine didn't even seem to remember that Carole was there. She was staring off into space. "Those were the happiest few weeks of my life," she said softly.

*Weeks?* Carole thought in confusion, wondering if she'd missed something again.

"We lost the baby before we were four months along," Lionel told Carole, reaching out to put a comforting arm around his wife's shoulder. "Miscarriage. Weird word, isn't it?"

"We tried again, of course." Nadine blinked hard a few times, her eyes still faraway and sad. "But a year passed, and then another, and still. . . . Well, we went to a specialist after a while, trying to figure out what was wrong. She told us there was practically no chance we'd ever have kids. So did the next doctor we went to. And the one after that. So finally we decided that maybe they were right and we'd just have to accept it."

Lionel nodded and gave Carole a small smile. "Sorry, I guess this isn't really a very cheerful story, is it?" he said. "But now you see why we care so much about Hometown Hope. It's the thing that really helped us get back on track. When we started volunteering, we realized that our own problems were really pretty minor compared to what a lot of other people go through every day. We really are lucky in most ways: We have our health, our jobs, our families and friends, and most of all each other. It helps us keep things in perspective when we feel sad about the way certain things have turned out."

"And it does more than that," Nadine added. "It makes us feel like we're doing some good in this world. Making a difference." She smiled at her husband. "Passing on a little bit of ourselves."

Carole had no idea what to say. Why were Lionel and Nadine telling her all this? It was making her more uncomfortable than ever.

"Lionel!" Craig Skippack called at that moment, waving at them from the playground. "Nadine! Yo! Can you give us a hand with this safety fence when you have a sec?"

"Be right there!" Nadine called back.

Lionel smiled at Carole as he and his wife stood and brushed the dirt off their knees. "Anyway, thanks for listening, Carole. We'll catch you later, okay?"

Carole was relieved when they'd left her alone once again with her work. *Good,* she thought, the couple's story fading as thoughts of Ben, Starlight, her job, and her father returned at full force. *Maybe now I can stop thinking about other people's problems and get back to the business of figuring out what to do about my own.*

# NINE

"You are certain this horse is pure Morgan?" Greta bluntly asked the short, portly man. "His chest looks rather narrow."

"Sure's I'm standing here," the barn manager drawled in response. He pushed back his wide-brimmed hat and shifted the toothpick he was chewing on from one corner of his mouth to the other as he blinked at the compact, handsome bay gelding standing in front of them. "Sire goes straight back to Bullrush. And check out that tail. Pretty nice, eh?"

Greta nodded shortly, barely sparing a glance for the horse's long, flowing dark tail before returning her gaze to its shoulders and forelegs.

Lisa had been feeling a little more relaxed ever since her stepmother's minivan had rolled to a stop at the small horse farm and the familiar sights and smells of horses had greeted her. In fact, she was actually enjoying watching her sister-in-law interrogate the barn manager. It was easy to forget that it was November, just days before Thanksgiving, as she stood in the sunshine of the warm California afternoon, watching the beautiful Morgan gelding prancing nervously in the farm's small, dusty paddock.

Meanwhile, Greta seemed to have forgotten that Lisa and Peter were there at all. She was all business, sizing up the Morgan with a practiced eye, running her hands down his legs and over his body. "All right," she said abruptly to the manager, stepping back. "I will need to see his gaits." She cast a long, slow look over the man's ample belly. "You can lead him for me? I will need to see him walk, trot, and canter. Briskly."

Before the man could answer, Lisa stepped forward. "I'll do it, Greta," she offered. "I can lead him around."

The manager gave her a suspicious glance. "You know anything about horses, young lady?"

Lisa ignored him. She was looking at her sister-in-law, who shrugged.

"All right," Greta said. "Many thanks, Lisa. Begin with the walk, if you please."

Lisa hid a smile as she stepped forward and took the Morgan's lead. Maybe Greta wasn't convinced Lisa knew much about horses, but it seemed she was willing to believe she knew at least a little.

For the next few minutes Lisa led the willing horse around and around the small paddock—

walk, trot, canter, trot again, then canter again, then back to the walk. Greta watched it all through narrowed eyes, never taking her eyes off the horse.

Finally she seemed satisfied. "That will do," she called to Lisa. She turned to the barn manager. "I will let you know my decision after I speak with my client."

Lisa guessed that meant Greta wasn't really interested in the horse. If she had been, she would have wanted to ride him, too. Lisa patted the Morgan on his gleaming neck, feeling a little sorry for him. The gelding snorted softly into her ear.

The man, too, seemed to realize what Greta's comment meant. He nodded, looking disappointed. "You wanted to see the chestnut, too, right? She's inside. Farrier just did her this noon, so I figured I'd leave 'er in for you."

"Fine." Greta nodded. "Let us go inside, then."

The manager led the way into the rustic log stable. As Lisa stepped over the threshold, she took a deep breath and glanced at Greta with a smile. "Mmm. I just love that smell, don't you?"

Greta cast her an uncertain glance. "I beg your pardon?"

"The smell," Lisa explained, suddenly feeling stupid. "You know—the smell of horses, the barn . . . It reminds me of Pine Hollow. Um, that's the stable where I ride back home."

"Ah." Greta turned away as the manager called them forward.

Lisa watched, her face burning, as her sister-in-law joined the manager at a stall. *How does she do it?* she wondered sourly. *How does she always manage to make me feel like a total idiot when all I'm trying to do is be nice?*

Taking a few deep breaths, she glanced over at her brother. Peter didn't seem to have noticed anything strange about their exchange. Looking at him also reminded Lisa of exactly why she was trying to get along with Greta in the first place. That helped her keep her temper as the three of them followed the manager to a stall near the end of the wide, clean-swept stable aisle. A young liver chestnut mare with a broad blaze was peering curiously out at them, her large eyes alert and intelligent.

This time, Greta looked much more impressed with the horse in question. After the manager had led the mare out for a quick inspection, Greta stepped back and nodded. "I would like to try this one, please," she said. "Where is her saddle?"

The manager waved to a stable hand who happened to be passing at that moment. A short time later, the mare was tacked up and walking quietly toward the paddock.

"Do you want me to lead her for you first?" Lisa asked Greta.

"Yes, thank you," Greta replied. She never took her eyes off the horse as she answered Lisa. "Halfway around at a walk, then a full circle at a trot, if you please."

Lisa nodded, grasping the mare's bridle. Lisa clucked to the horse and they got moving. When she returned, a little breathless from the exercise, Greta looked more pleased than ever.

"Very nice," she muttered. She glanced at the manager. "But the faster gaits are equally important in this case."

Lisa patted the mare, who seemed to have a sweet temperament to match her healthy good looks. "I could take her around a few times," she suggested, suddenly very eager to climb into a saddle again. "That way you could watch someone else riding her before you get on her yourself."

Greta shook her head immediately. "I will ride her myself," she said firmly. Without further hesitation, she walked up to the mare, gave her a quick pat, and then swung herself up into the saddle in one smooth movement.

Lisa felt a little stung by Greta's quick dismissal. But as she watched her sister-in-law ride the mare across the paddock, she had to admit that Greta was an excellent rider.

Lisa leaned on the paddock gate beside Peter, both of them watching as Greta trotted the horse along the fence line, testing its gaits. The manager hurried after Greta on the other side of the fence, calling out helpful suggestions, which Greta ignored.

Peter smiled, his eyes never leaving his new wife. "She's a good rider, isn't she?" he commented. "I mean, I really don't know much about these things, but everyone tells me she is."

"She's an amazing rider." Lisa hesitated, not sure how to say what she wanted to say next without making Peter feel as if she wasn't totally on his side. "Er, but not only that. She's really . . . different," she offered at last. "Very colorful."

"I know. Isn't she great?" Peter sighed and rested his chin on one hand as he leaned against the fence and watched Greta. "As soon as I met her, I knew she was something special. I mean, she's smart, she's beautiful, she's just as interested in languages as I am, she's a terrific mother. . . ."

Lisa had almost forgotten about Dieter and Hanni again. She stood up straight and looked at her brother, wondering how he really felt about them. "Well," she said carefully, "I guess it all must still be kind of, well, challenging. I mean, a new wife from a whole other country, new stepkids . . ."

Peter shrugged. "Yeah, I suppose it's sort of a big change in some ways. To tell the truth, the kids and I are taking a little longer to get used to each other than I expected." He frowned slightly, then shrugged again. "Still, I guess that's the way in any new situation, right? Period of adjustment. Anyway, now that I'm their stepdad and not just Mama's boyfriend, I'm sure we'll get into the swing of being a real family soon."

Lisa thought that sounded a little naive, but she didn't say so. "Love conquers all, right?" she said lightly.

"Not just love. Marriage takes work, too," Peter said solemnly, sounding so much like their father that Lisa turned to look at him, assuring herself that it was still Peter standing beside her. "Hard work, on both sides. And Greta and I are definitely ready to work as hard as we need to at this." His gaze strayed to his wife again.

Lisa turned to watch Greta, too, thinking about what Peter had said. Despite his speech about hard work, she still wasn't totally convinced that he was being realistic about his new family. Lisa hadn't seen any signs that her brother and Greta's kids were making any real efforts to adjust to each other at all. And if Greta's attitude toward Peter's family was any indication, they weren't going to be getting much help from her.

"Oh well," Lisa said, her mind wandering back to her own immediate family. Her mother hadn't been much help after the divorce, and her father had moved to California almost immediately after the breakup, so he hadn't exactly been available to help Lisa get through it. And somehow they had all survived. "I guess by now we're all pretty much experts at adjusting to new family situations."

Peter glanced at her. "You mean Evelyn?" he said. "Yeah, it's still weird thinking about Dad having a new wife, isn't it?"

Lisa hadn't been thinking of Evelyn in particular, but she nodded. "I guess so, a little," she agreed. "But it helps a lot that she's so friendly and nice."

She winced as soon as the words left her mouth, hoping that Peter didn't think she was implying that Evelyn was nicer and friendlier than Greta. But Peter didn't seem to catch on to the comparison. He was nodding slowly. "You know, Lisa, I have to hand it to you," he commented. "You and Evelyn really seem to get along great. I have to admit, I still have a little trouble being around her, thinking of her as part of the family or whatever." He kicked at the base of the fence post. "It's going to be weird seeing her at the Thanksgiving table this year instead of Mom."

*I guess that's true,* Lisa thought, leaning against the fence again and gazing into the paddock, where Greta was cantering the chestnut mare in a tight circle. *But that's definitely not the only thing that's going to be weird about Thanksgiving this year.*

———

At that moment, Stevie was leaning against a fence watching half a dozen elderly horses grazing beneath the gray, chilly Virginia sky. "Brr!" she commented, pulling her fleece jacket closer around her neck. "It's really starting to feel like Thanksgiving out here, isn't it?"

Deborah nodded. Then she turned to Mrs. Monroe. "Your farm is lovely," she said politely.

"Why, thank you, dear." Mrs. Monroe waved one arm to indicate the grazing horses. "There you have it—my dear old residents. Aren't they beautiful?"

"Absolutely," Deborah replied.

Stevie had to agree with that. There was a small barren paddock between where they were standing and the large pasture where the horses were grazing, but two of the horses were close enough to the fence for Stevie to get a pretty good look at them. One appeared to be a Thoroughbred mare, and the other was an enormous warmblood gelding, nearly seventeen hands high, with a funny snip on his huge bay face that looked like a cat's head—at least from Stevie's viewpoint.

"What's his name?" Stevie asked Mrs. Monroe, pointing to the bay.

Mrs. Monroe looked where she was pointing. "Hmmm? Oh, the warmblood? His name is Leo. He was quite a good show jumper in his younger days. Belongs to a fellow who lives just outside of

Boston—excellent rider, but no room for old soldiers like Leo, so he called me to take him in. Isn't he handsome?"

Before Stevie could answer, there was a sudden flurry of barking from somewhere behind the barn. "What's that?" Deborah asked, looking startled.

"Oh dear." Mrs. Monroe was already hurrying in the direction of the noise. "Sounds like the pups have gotten loose again. I'll be back in a jiff."

"Do you need any help?" Stevie asked uncertainly.

Mrs. Monroe waved one hand cheerily. "No, no, dear," she called over her shoulder. "They're just small dogs. I'll be fine."

When the woman had disappeared around the corner, Stevie blew out a sigh and turned to Deborah. "Whew!" she exclaimed. "And people say *I* talk a lot!"

Deborah laughed. "I'm really sorry, Stevie," she said. "I knew this wasn't going to be thrilling, but I never dreamed it would be quite as dull as this. When she gets back, I'm going to do my best to get us out of here as quickly as possible."

"Maybe we should make a run for it now," Stevie suggested. But she was only joking. Glancing out at the pasture again, she found her gaze drawn back to Leo. Even though hollows were visible above his eyes and his back was swayed slightly

144

with age, she could see the outline of the majestic young competitor he had once been.

"Actually," Deborah said with a grimace, picking at a splinter on the fence in front of her, "just about the only thing more boring than this interview is going to be the story I have to write about it. Mrs. Monroe really hasn't given me one bit of information I can use, unless I want to turn it into an article about her sister and all the boyfriends she had back before the war."

Stevie sighed, still watching Leo as he grazed. "You know, it's kind of a shame," she said. "I mean, no matter how dull she is, this woman is performing a really great service here. In her own older years, she's providing a safe, loving home for horses that might not have anywhere to go otherwise. And didn't you hear what she said? People are sending their retirees to her from places as far away as Boston!"

Deborah nodded, looking slightly sheepish. "I know, you're right," she said. "I just wish there was a way to get all that good stuff across to the readers. Then it might actually make a readable article."

"Isn't it obvious?" Stevie grinned. "You've got to forget about Mrs. Monroe and her sister and her cats and all the rest of it. Focus on the horses! Find out more about the ones here, where they came from, that kind of thing. They're the reason for this place, right? And anything about horses is at least *slightly* interesting—at least, that's what Carole always tells us."

Deborah sighed. "Actually, I was thinking along those lines myself. The only trouble is, it means sticking around this place a little longer . . . and trying to drag that kind of information out of Mrs. Monroe in between still more stories about her childhood and the family farm and who knows what else."

"You can do it," Stevie said confidently. "Don't tell me nice old Mrs. Monroe scares you more as an interview subject than that horrible Central American drug lord you tackled last year. Or the tobacco executive you exposed before that. Or—"

"Okay, okay, you've made your point." Deborah chuckled and clapped Stevie on the shoulder. "I knew there was a reason I brought you along! You're even better at this motivation stuff than my editor at the paper."

"So we're sticking around?"

Deborah nodded. "We don't leave until we get our story. You have my word."

The two of them spent the next few minutes watching the horses in the pasture and discussing questions Deborah could ask. Finally Mrs. Monroe hurried toward them again, huffing and puffing.

"There we are, dears," she said. "Ready to go inside and warm up with another cup of tea?"

146

"Thank you, but not quite yet," Deborah replied politely. "Actually, I was hoping we could get a closer look at some of your residents. Are there any horses in the barn we could meet?"

"Oh, that seems like a lot of trouble for you," Mrs. Monroe demurred. "Why don't we just go inside and get comfortable? It's a bit nippy out here, and I wouldn't want you young girls to catch a chill."

"Oh, we're not cold," Stevie said helpfully. "It's very refreshing."

Deborah nodded. "Besides, it will be warmer inside the barn," she pointed out. "We can start there and give ourselves a chance to warm up a bit while we see the horses inside."

"Well, yes." Mrs. Monroe was starting to look flustered. "But you see, I can tell you anything you need to know about my horses. I know everything about them—that way I can give each one the care it needs, you know."

"That's very commendable." Deborah smiled at the woman, but Stevie detected steely determination in her face. "But really, I think the article will be better if I can just check out a few of the horses myself. You know—it will give it that personal touch that people like."

Stevie felt a twinge of pity for Mrs. Monroe as she sighed heavily and gave in, gesturing for the visitors to follow her as she headed across the yard

147

toward the barn once again. *Poor old lady,* Stevie thought with a secret smile. *She's probably regretting ever asking Deborah here now that she's making her run all over the farm to show her around.*

Still, Stevie knew that Mrs. Monroe couldn't be all that feeble if she took care of half a dozen or more horses by herself. Even geriatric horses needed to be fed, watered, and groomed, and to have their stalls cleaned.

*She probably just didn't want to be bothered,* Stevie thought as she followed the two women into the barn, which was large and brightly lit. *She probably loves the idea of sipping tea and blabbing some more about her wonderful family and all that. I guess that was her idea of what being interviewed should be like.*

Obviously, though, it wasn't what Deborah had in mind, and Stevie was glad about that. Because of Deborah's polite but firm insistence on doing things her way, the article would turn out a lot better. That meant more people would learn about Mrs. Monroe's farm, and more good horses would be helped in the long run. That was worth upsetting an old woman a little bit, wasn't it?

Inside the barn, Stevie couldn't help noticing that every one of the first few stalls they passed was swept clean. She was impressed—the dirt floors and cement walls were as spotless as if a horse hadn't set foot in them in ages. She guessed they had caught the woman on a day when she'd decided to air out the stalls, changing all the old bedding for fresh rather than simply replacing the soiled portions. Even so, Stevie was glad that Max wasn't there to see it. He was always complaining about her stall-cleaning technique, which very rarely involved scrubbing down the walls or sweeping up every last scrap of straw before bringing in the new bedding, even on an airing-out day.

"Wow," she said as she caught up with Mrs. Monroe, who was chattering to Deborah about the approaching Thanksgiving holiday. "This place is so clean. Do you do all the mucking out yourself?"

Mrs. Monroe looked startled. "Why, no, dear, of course not." She laughed. "I'm just an old woman; how could I possibly do all that? There's a neighbor boy who helps out after school. He's a dear—so good with the horses, and he really appreciates the pocket money."

Before long the three of them were standing in front of a roomy box stall near the entrance. Inside, a swaybacked gray gelding blinked sleepily at them through eyes partly clouded with cataracts; he moved forward slowly and accepted their pats impassively.

"This is Edison," Mrs. Monroe said. "He's thirty-three years young."

"Wow." Stevie scratched the old horse beneath

his mane. "And I thought Nero was ancient when he died last year at twenty-nine."

Deborah stroked Edison's nose and smiled at Mrs. Monroe. "Nero was one of the horses at my husband's riding stable," she explained. "I'm impressed that your charges can live to such a grand old age."

"Oh, yes," Mrs. Monroe said complacently. "The horses just love living here. And I love having them around. Why, Edison here is quite a character. Just the other day he was romping in the pasture with the others and jabbed his foot with a stone. That's why he's resting in his stall this week."

Stevie nodded. "The vet recommended keeping him in?"

Mrs. Monroe smiled vaguely. "Hmmm? Well, you know what they say—no foot, no horse. Now, would you like to hear a bit more of old Edison's history? He's one of my favorites, you know—used to be a lead pony at a racetrack in Florida until he got too old to keep up. He was such an old dear that his owners knew he would be just perfect for a riding center for disabled children. So that was his next job—did it for nigh on eight years after retiring from the track. Then the cataracts started, and they knew he couldn't do that anymore, but they couldn't bear to put him down. So the parents of one of the children—wealthy people who appreciated all Edison had done for their boy—agreed to pay to ship him here, send a check every six months for his room and board. And no wonder. Why, the stories they tell of how Edison helped their child, I believe his name is Bruce, could just bring a tear to your eye—"

"Yes, I see," Deborah interrupted. "That's very interesting. Now, perhaps you could fill me in on a few of your other—"

"Oh! I almost forgot!" Mrs. Monroe laughed and clapped her hands. "I haven't told you how Edison got his name. You see, there was this one racehorse who was afraid of the dark, and—"

"I'm sorry to interrupt," Deborah said, her voice a little louder. "But I'm afraid Stevie and I are on a tight schedule today. Maybe you could tell us more about Edison another time. Right now, I think we'd really better move on to some of the others."

Mrs. Monroe looked taken aback. "Oh, I see," she said. "Well, if you like, I could phone you later when you have more time and give you the rest of the information."

"No, no, we do have a few more minutes right now." Deborah smiled appeasingly and put one hand on the woman's arm. "And while Edison is just wonderful, I'd really like to meet a few of the other horses. For the story, you know."

Mrs. Monroe shook her head. "Oh, dear. You

see, the others are all outside," she said. "Horses love to graze, you know. I'm afraid we'd never catch up to them all."

"We don't need to see them all," Deborah conceded. "Perhaps just one?"

"How about that big bay?" Stevie put in. "Leo. He looks like a nice old guy. I'm sure I could catch him and lead him in—all I need is a halter." Spotting several well-worn halters hanging on a hook nearby, she hurried toward them and grabbed one and a lead. "Here, this one looks like it's big enough."

"Oh dear." Mrs. Monroe looked worried. "I'm not sure this is a good idea. What if he hurts you? Or—"

"You don't have to worry," Deborah interrupted. "Stevie's very experienced. And Leo looked like a calm old fellow."

"Well . . ." Mrs. Monroe still looked reluctant, though Stevie couldn't imagine why.

*It's not as if she has to do anything,* she thought. Then she smiled, suddenly remembering that her grandmother could be the same way whenever someone else dared to take charge of the day's plans. *I guess Mrs. M's just like Grandma Jean,* Stevie added to herself. *She never thinks anything's a good idea unless she thinks of it herself.*

"Back in a minute," Stevie sang out, hurrying toward the door with the halter before Mrs.

Monroe could protest further. She only hoped Deborah would forgive her for leaving her alone with the woman's stories.

Outside, Stevie vaulted easily over the wire-backed paddock fence and hurried toward the pasture fence. Leo was still grazing just a few yards beyond the fence line, and he lifted his head to watch as Stevie ducked between the boards of the fence and straightened up.

"Hey there, big boy," she called in a friendly voice. "How's it going?"

She walked slowly toward Leo with the halter tucked behind her back, admiring the huge horse's long, clean legs and muscular hindquarters. His back was slightly swayed, as she'd noticed earlier, and now that she was closer she could see that he wasn't quite as fit and full-bodied as he appeared from a distance. Still, he looked awfully good for a horse his age, and it was easy to see the athlete that he once was.

Stevie continued to approach Leo slowly, speaking softly to him the whole time. The old horse pricked his ears toward her curiously and let out a gentle snort.

"That's it, Leo baby," Stevie murmured. "I just want to take you for a little walk, okay?"

As she reached the horse's side and put out her hand to pat him, Stevie noticed that a bit of partly chewed food was dribbling out of one side of his mouth. At first she thought nothing of it—when Belle was distracted, she often dropped bits of whatever she was chewing at the time.

But then Leo tossed his head and flicked out his tongue, releasing another wad of greenish goo. Stevie frowned as something tugged at the back of her mind. Why did the sight of that slimy bit of half-chewed grass make her feel strangely anxious?

Just then the horse nickered, and Stevie's attention snapped back to him. "It's all right, old boy," she crooned. "We just want to say hello. What do you say?"

The horse lowered his huge head, his nostrils working as he snuffled at her face and hair. A moment later Stevie was patting his neck with one hand and reaching up to slip the halter onto his big head with the other. Leo stood calmly until she clucked to him and stepped forward; then he followed along placidly.

"That's a good boy," Stevie said. "Come on, we're just going right over here." She aimed for Deborah and Mrs. Monroe, who were standing just inside the pasture fence near the gate.

As she headed toward them, Stevie felt something wet plop onto her shoulder, ooze over the collar of her jacket, and drip on her bare neck. She frowned again as she reached up to wipe it away. Her fingers came back green. Raising them to get a better look, she saw partly smashed blades of grass and bits of clover.

"Hmmm," she said. "Looks like you're having a little trouble chewing."

Suddenly it came to her: Judy Barker's voice saying, *Problems can be worse in older horses whose teeth are in poor shape.* And her own voice, reciting what Max had always taught her: *If there's a wad of grass or hay that isn't chewed up all the way, it sort of moves down the horse's throat in a wad. If it gets stuck in the esophagus, it's called choke. And if it makes it farther down and can't be digested right, it means impaction colic, which can require surgery.*

"Yikes," Stevie said softly, stopping and turning to stare at the old horse. Could he be having serious dental problems? How was that possible? Surely Mrs. Monroe or her vet would have made the diagnosis long before it reached a dangerous point. . . .

Leo swung his big head around to look at her. His mouth moved, and his tongue flicked out again, spattering bits of grass around him.

That was all the encouragement Stevie needed. Dropping the lead, she pried his mouth open. "It's okay, boy," she murmured. "I just want to take a look."

"What are you doing, dear?" Mrs. Monroe's voice floated toward her.

Stevie glanced up just long enough to see that

the woman was hurrying in her direction with Deborah on her heels. Mrs. Monroe's normally cheerful face wore a frown, and she was moving faster than Stevie had seen her move all day.

"I think he may be having a problem with his teeth," Stevie explained as the two women reached her. "He's quidding up a storm, and that can lead to serious health problems, like—"

"Nonsense!" Mrs. Monroe laughed. "It's not his teeth. He just likes to play with his food, that's all. Nothing serious at all."

Stevie frowned. "I really don't think—" she began worriedly.

"Listen, young lady," Mrs. Monroe snapped testily. "I've been caring for horses for more years than you've been alive. Now, Leo is just fine. Why don't we go inside and discuss it?"

"But he's quidding," Stevie said stubbornly. "You really should at least ask your vet to take a look. He may need to have his teeth floated more often."

"Nonsense," the woman replied. "I know my horses. They're fine. They get the best care available."

"Now, just a minute," Deborah broke in, looking very interested. "We're not accusing you of anything here, Mrs. Monroe. But Stevie seems quite concerned about this horse, and—"

"There's no reason for concern," Mrs. Monroe said quickly. "The horse is just fine."

At that moment, Leo made a loud slurping sound and opened his mouth. A large wad of green gook dribbled out, and he tossed his head with a snort. Now Stevie was positive that something was wrong. "If you don't call a vet, I will," she said firmly. "This horse needs to be checked out, and the sooner the better."

Mrs. Monroe looked outraged. "How dare you!" she huffed. "Just because a horse is a sloppy eater, it doesn't mean there's a problem."

"Is that what you're claiming the problem is here?" Deborah asked sharply. Stevie noticed that she had her notebook in her hand and was scribbling notes even as she spoke. "Because I'd be very interested in hearing the owner's comments on such an interesting quirk. I'd also love to hear what your vet says about Leo's teeth."

Stevie stared at Leo as Deborah continued to shoot questions at Mrs. Monroe, asking about the medical and dental care given to her horses. She was in shock. How could a woman who seemed so nice and caring neglect something as important as a horse's teeth? And if she was letting that slide, what other corners might she be cutting on her charges' care?

". . . and to convince me of that, I would want to see your medical and financial records for this place, proving that the care you promised the owners has been provided and properly paid for," Deborah was saying when Stevie tuned back in to the conversation.

"Well, I never!" Mrs. Monroe's face was bright crimson, and her fists were clenched at her sides. "The impudence! I want you both off my property—now!"

Stevie opened her mouth to protest. She didn't want to leave until she was sure Leo—and the other horses—were okay. But Deborah clamped a hand firmly on her arm.

"Fine," Deborah replied coolly, dragging Stevie toward the paddock gate. "But this isn't the last you'll be hearing of this. You can count on that."

"But Deborah!" Stevie whispered as the reporter marched her toward the car. "Leo—"

"Don't worry, he won't be under that woman's care for long," Deborah replied in a low voice. She glanced over her shoulder as Stevie opened the passenger door and slid inside. Hurrying around to the driver's side, Deborah hopped in and started the engine, barely pausing long enough to put on her seat belt. "Besides, I think there's more than a few late dental appointments going on here. Didn't you see the way she got all defensive back there when I started asking real questions?"

Stevie glanced at Deborah. The reporter's face was shining, and her eyes were glittering as she steered the car back onto the road. "Wow," Stevie commented, forgetting about Leo's teeth for a second. "Look at you. You're, like, *glowing!*"

Deborah laughed, sounding a little embarrassed. "I guess I am a little excited," she confessed. "Here I thought this would be the dullest story I ever wrote, and what do you know? We stumble onto what could be a real scam!"

"We're going to make sure Leo gets some help, right?" Stevie was feeling a twinge of excitement mixed with her concern. Deborah's enthusiasm was infectious.

"Right. Leo and all the animals on that woman's property." Checking her rearview mirror, Deborah pulled off to the side of the quiet country road. Leaning over to Stevie's side of the car, she yanked open the glove compartment and grabbed her cell phone. "But we've got to work fast, before she starts covering things up. I'm going to make a few quick calls right now."

TEN

Lisa stared out the window of the minivan, wondering if a jury would really convict her for strangling two screaming kids. Especially when they were screaming in German.

Squeezing her eyes shut, she prayed they would reach the showgrounds soon, before she went completely insane. "Dieter! Hanni!" Greta exclaimed, turning around from her seat beside Peter, who was driving. "Hush, darlings. We will be there soon." She glanced at Lisa with a slight frown. "Can you not keep them entertained for just a few minutes, Lisa?"

"Apparently not," Lisa muttered. She glared at her sister-in-law, but Greta had already turned around again and was chattering at Peter in German. Lisa blew out a frustrated sigh, feeling very alone. Her father and Evelyn had both declined to come to the horse show—her father had claimed he needed to go into the office for a few hours, and

Evelyn had decided it would be too long and tiring a trip for Lily.

"Lisa! Lisa!" Hanni bounced up and down in her seat. "Lisa! Sing us a song."

"Hey! What happened to your seat belt?" Lisa leaned over to strap the little girl in again.

Meanwhile, Dieter poked her in the back. "Sing us a song," he demanded. "Sing!"

Lisa scowled. The last thing she felt like doing was singing. She was seriously wishing she'd never agreed to go to the horse show. Still, there wasn't much she could do about that at the moment. Taking a deep breath, she launched into her best rendition of "Tomorrow," which she knew well from acting in a local production of *Annie* years earlier.

Within seconds, Hanni and Dieter were giggling loudly. They started shrieking to each other in some strange amalgamation of English, German, and French, finally getting so loud that Lisa broke off in midnote.

"What!" she demanded. "Or should I ask that question in French?" She promptly did so, dredging up everything she'd learned in several years of studying the language in school and adding a few choice French words about the proper behavior of young children in an automobile.

"Mama! Mama!" Dieter shouted. "Lisa's going crazy!"

Hanni giggled. "*Oui*, Mama!" she cried. "She's speaking some strange language. We can't understand her!"

Greta turned around again, smiling indulgently at her children. "Now, now, *Liebling!*" she exclaimed. "Do not make Lisa feel bad because her accent is not *richtig*, all right?"

Lisa frowned as the children giggled and shot her amused looks. She was starting to get the feeling that it was going to be a very long day.

"Forget it, baby." Stevie yanked Belle's head away from a patch of weeds near the back paddock. "You know what that stuff does to you. No way am I letting you fall off the wagon."

Belle shook her head, looking disgruntled, as Stevie led her on past the temptation of the weed patch. The mare was allergic to several varieties of weeds, and while Max and the rest of the Pine Hollow staff did their best to keep the area clear and mowed, a few weeds invariably escaped their attention and flourished here and there. It was always a challenge for Stevie to keep her horse from sampling them as they passed, and that day was no exception. The two of them had just finished a nice long workout in the schooling ring, practicing with the cavalletti left there from Max's last lesson with the intermediate riding class, and despite the strenuous exercise, Belle was still feisty as Stevie walked her around the stable building to cool her down.

"You know," Stevie commented to the horse, giving her a solid pat on the neck, "I do believe that you are probably the most excellent horse in the entire barn. Maybe even in the entire world."

As they rounded the corner, Stevie spotted Deborah's car. Instead of turning up the drive toward the house, it came to a stop in the gravel parking area in front of the stable.

Leo and the rest of the horses at Mrs. Monroe's farm hadn't been far from Stevie's thoughts since Deborah had dropped her off at her home the previous afternoon. "Come on," Stevie told her horse, tugging gently on her lead to change directions. "Let's go talk to Deborah for a minute."

Trailing her horse behind her, Stevie hurried toward Deborah's car. The reporter waved as she climbed out of the driver's seat. "Hi, Stevie!" she called. Her eyes looked tired and her auburn hair was gathered into a sloppy ponytail. Stevie guessed she had been working almost nonstop since the day before—she looked that way herself when she'd been up most of the night writing a paper or studying for a test. "I was hoping you'd be here."

"So what happened?" Stevie demanded anxiously. "Did you shut her down?"

Deborah laughed ruefully as she pushed her car door shut. "It's only been twenty-four hours,

163

Stevie," she said. "It's going to take a little more time than that, I'm afraid. But the authorities are on the job, so it shouldn't be long now."

"Good." Stevie nodded. "Are you still going to write an article about this?"

Deborah looked surprised that she was even asking. "Of course!" she exclaimed. "This is a great story. It could really do some good—let people know they need to be careful about who they get to care for their animals." She grimaced. "Besides, I've been doing some digging on our dear old friend Mrs. Monroe, and she's had quite a nice little scam going up there at her farm for a while now."

Belle shoved her nose at Stevie's arm, and Stevie patted the mare absently. She was focused on what Deborah was telling her. "What do you mean?" she asked. "What was she doing?"

"Well, from what I've been able to find out so far, she was doing more than just skimping on her residents' medical care." Deborah shook her head. "She was basically doing everything she could to squeeze the maximum amount of money out of her business. First of all, she made a point of seeking out her boarders from places that were too far away or from people who were too busy to check up on their horses very much. The kind of people who weren't likely to drop by unannounced. Then she'd give the horses the bare minimum of care—minus most meds and special treatments."

"Including routine dental care," Stevie murmured, thinking again of Leo. "That's totally . . . um . . ." She searched her mind for a word that would be strong enough to describe what she thought of Mrs. Monroe's actions.

"Despicable?" Deborah offered. "Unconscionable? Abhorrent?"

"Something like that," Stevie agreed, "but worse. So is there more?"

Deborah sighed and smoothed back a stray strand of hair that the chilly breeze had blown into her face. "I'm afraid so," she said. "More of the same, really. Some of the owners signed up for various expensive extras—special grain mixes, extra exercise, supplements and vitamins, eyewashes and other special health treatments, and so forth. Did the horses ever see any of that? All evidence so far indicates that they didn't. Oh, and by the way—remember those nice clean stalls?"

Stevie nodded. "Don't tell me. She made the horses sweep them out themselves?" she joked weakly.

"Hardly," Deborah replied. "The horses weren't allowed near those stalls. Only the really old and infirm ever came inside, like old Edison, for instance. Almost all the owners paid for stall boarding, but most of the horses got little more than bare-bones field boarding."

Stevie was shocked. She knew there was nothing wrong with field boarding a horse, even an older horse. But she also knew that keeping a horse in a stall cost a stable much more in time and work, which meant a much higher monthly boarding fee. Also, Mrs. Monroe's clients were most likely paying her the extra money to keep a close eye on their horses—many of whom probably had health problems because of their advanced age, such as Leo's dental troubles. There was no way the woman could have been doing that if she didn't handle the horses every day by bringing them inside. And it sounded as though she really didn't care about any of that.

Stevie's mind was reeling with everything Deborah had just told her. "It's so horrible," she said. "And just think, we almost walked in and out of there without even noticing anything was wrong."

"I know." Deborah took a step closer and put a hand on Stevie's shoulder, looking very serious. "I really want to thank you for that, actually. I was so busy hating the assignment I was given that I almost missed out on the real story. I might have walked away and written a polite little human-interest piece that would've made even more people send their horses to her." She smiled. "But luckily, you were there to guilt me into staying—

and alert enough to spot Leo's problems, which was the hint we needed to uncover the rest."

Stevie felt good about Deborah's praise. Now that she thought about it, she realized she really was at least partly responsible for bringing Mrs. Monroe's deception to light. "Thanks," she said modestly. "But you were the one who did all the rest of the uncovering. How'd you find out so much info in such a short time, anyway?"

"Oh, a reporter has her ways," Deborah said mischievously. She winked. "For instance, remember that neighbor boy Mrs. Monroe mentioned?"

"You mean the one she claimed helped out around the barn after school?"

Deborah nodded grimly. "Well, I tracked him down, and boy, did he have some stories to tell," she said. "She actually did hire him occasionally, I think mostly because he's only fourteen and would work hard for less than minimum wage. Mrs. Monroe would bring him over to clean up the place occasionally—muck out the pastures, clean the watering troughs, mow down the weeds, things like that. Also, when a new potential boarder came to inspect the place, or on the rare occasion when an owner wanted to stop by and visit his or her horse, she would have the boy fix things up to look a little more legit." She shrugged. "I'm sure she would've done the same before our visit, except that she seemed to think we'd be satisfied with a nice chat over tea and a quick glance at the pasture."

Stevie grinned. "Little did she know."

But her grin faded quickly. The things Deborah was telling her really weren't anything to smile about. As Belle nudged her again, leaving a bit of drool dripping down her neck, Stevie flashed back to poor Leo, dribbling his food because he couldn't chew it properly. No wonder he had looked a little underweight—how long ago had his problem begun to develop? And how much longer would it have gone on if Stevie and Deborah hadn't happened by? Probably until the old gelding died of colic or other complications. . . .

"It's so weird, you know?" Stevie said, burying her hands in Belle's thick, dark mane as a wave of intense anger passed through her. "Mrs. Monroe looked like someone's old granny, and yet she turns out to be, like, evil."

"Evil?" Deborah repeated. "No, I don't think so."

Stevie couldn't believe her ears. "What do you mean? She totally neglects helpless old horses just to make a little more money. What could be more evil than that?"

Deborah sighed. "I know what you're saying. But *evil* is a pretty strong word. Look at it this way: If you or I or Max or anyone else here at Pine Hollow did the things Mrs. Monroe did, then yes,

I would say that was evil, because we all know better." She reached over and gently stroked Belle's soft nose. "But I'm not sure Mrs. Monroe really understood what was so wrong about her actions. Yes, she was definitely ignorant and greedy. She knew she was cutting corners, and that makes her dishonest. But it doesn't necessarily make her *evil*. Not really."

Stevie didn't see the difference, but she shrugged. "I don't care what you want to call it, as long as someone takes those horses away and punishes her for what she did."

"Oh, don't worry about that," Deborah said. "She's going to pay. But better than that—she's going to be an example. When this article runs in the paper, a lot of people will read it. And maybe some of them are making ignorant or greedy decisions about animals themselves. And maybe, just maybe, they'll learn a little something from Mrs. Monroe's example. That may help another horse somewhere." She smiled. "That's the great thing about what I do. You never know when your words are going to touch someone in a really important way."

"Wow. I never thought of it like that." Stevie was a little awed at the thought. Somewhere out there, a horse—maybe lots of horses—could have a better life, just because she'd noticed some green slime falling out of Leo's mouth. It was pretty amazing, really. "No wonder you love your job."

"I do love it." Deborah glanced at her watch and sighed. "But I don't love the deadlines. And I've got a major one now. My editor wants this story on his desk by nine P.M., and I've barely started writing." She reached into her pocket and fished out a crumpled piece of notebook paper. "Actually, I just started making a few notes for the opening paragraph at stoplights on my way over here from the county commissioner's office. Would you mind if I ran the first few sentences by you?"

"No problem!" Stevie said quickly.

Deborah flattened out the paper on the hood of her car. Then she cleared her throat. "All right," she said. "Remember that this is rough. 'On a quiet country lane, it has been business as usual for—' No, wait," Deborah interrupted herself with a frown. "That doesn't sound right. Maybe it should be more like, 'On a quiet country lane, a certain businesswoman has been going quietly about her business for many years. However . . .' Hmmm. No, that's not quite right, either." She frowned at the scrap of paper in her hand.

Stevie leaned against Belle, thinking hard about what Deborah had just read. "That stuff all sounds okay," she said slowly. "But at the risk of sounding like Carole here, don't you think it might be better to talk about the horses right from the beginning? You know, make the point about how horrible this scam really was, like maybe, 'The average horse is more than a thousand pounds of muscle, sinew, and bone. And yet without the care of a responsible person, he is as helpless as a baby.' Then blah, blah, blah, and on to Mrs. Monroe."

Deborah's eyes widened. "That's great!" she exclaimed, digging into her pocket again. "Wait, don't forget that. I want to get it down." She finally located the stub of a pencil in her back pocket and scribbled down a few lines on the back of her original notes. Then she held it up, reading it over silently. "This is great," she announced after a moment. "Stevie, you're a genius!"

"I try," Stevie said modestly. She could hardly believe Deborah might actually want to use her suggestion in her article. "Do you really like it?"

"I love it," Deborah assured her. "I want to use it as the opener for the article—if you don't mind, that is. In fact, now that I think about it, maybe you deserve a co-byline on this thing." She smiled and winked. "I mean, not only did you start off the investigation, but now you're starting off the writing, too! I could ask my editor to add a line at the beginning, maybe something like 'By Deborah Hale, with special reporting by Stephanie Lake.'"

Stevie's jaw dropped. "Are you serious?" she

171

cried. "My name in the paper? That would be so totally, amazingly cool!"

"Yeah." Deborah smiled at her as she tucked her notes back into her pocket. "Extremely cool."

"Hanni!" Lisa said sharply. "Don't touch that."

The little girl drew back from a large pile of fresh manure, shooting Lisa a dirty look. Then she hurried over to her brother, who was staring at a sleeping corgi nearby, and whispered something in his ear, making them both laugh.

Lisa rolled her eyes and sighed. "I don't know why she bothers to whisper," she told Peter. "It's not like I can understand most of what they say anyway, when they keep switching back and forth between their twenty-seven different languages."

Peter smiled sympathetically. "I know how you feel," he said as they strolled after the kids. "Did you know they speak a little Polish? Apparently their grandmother taught them. I didn't understand a word of it when I first met Greta." He laughed. "Luckily, though, I've picked up quite a bit in the past couple of months. So if they want to keep fooling me, they'll have to start learning Swahili or Urdu."

Lisa smiled. As annoying as Greta's children were, she was actually feeling pretty good. It was hard to feel totally terrible while she was at a horse show, especially on such a gorgeous autumn day.

Or rather, the Southern California version of autumn, which as far as Lisa could tell was just like the Southern California version of every other season—warm, sunny, and pleasant. Besides that, it was nice to finally have some time to just chat with her brother, catching up on each other's lives, as they'd been doing ever since Greta had hurried off to her first meeting. Even the presence of Greta's kids couldn't totally ruin that.

"Hey, I'm sure you could catch on even if they started learning Outer Mongolian or something," Lisa told her brother with a laugh. "You've always been so great at languages."

"Thanks." Peter smiled. "It's easy to be good at what you love. Like you and Greta with your riding, you know?"

Lisa shrugged. "I guess you're right about that," she agreed, glancing around the showgrounds. The horse show was just a small local event, but it was as busy and exciting as every show she'd ever attended, from the regular schooling shows at Pine Hollow to the American Horse Show. All around her, riders were bustling back and forth, leading horses, carrying tack or grooming tools, attaching armbands, chattering anxiously with each other about judges, courses, and strategies. Just then the PA system crackled to life, announcing that the first class would be starting in ten minutes. It made Lisa's heart beat a little faster just hearing the announcement, even though she was only there as a spectator. "Come on," she told Peter. "Let's go find seats so we can watch."

He nodded and called to Dieter and Hanni. The kids looked irritated at the interruption, but they trailed along as Lisa and Peter headed for the bleachers that overlooked the main ring. Soon all four of them were seated in an empty row.

Hanni's gaze was drawn to the competitors warming up just outside the ring. But Dieter started fidgeting almost immediately.

Peter frowned at him. "Dieter, it's time to sit quietly now for a while, all right? We all want to watch the first event. Would you like a hot dog or something before it gets started?"

"Bleagh. I hate hot dogs," Dieter declared, making a retching sound and pretending to throw up.

Peter frowned. "Dieter!" he said sharply. "That's enough. I'm certainly not going to force you to eat a hot dog, or watch the show, for that matter. But I do think you need to be polite while the rest of us are enjoying ourselves."

Dieter rolled his eyes. "Whatever," he muttered, sounding so much like any American kid that Lisa almost smiled.

Peter didn't seem particularly amused. "Dieter!" he said warningly. "Don't push it, kiddo. Do you hear me?"

By now, Hanni was paying more attention to

their conversation than to the horses. "Of course he hears you," she put in, making a face at Peter. "You're talking loud enough for the whole world to hear."

"Enough, Hanni!" Peter rounded on her. "You're not helping."

Hanni responded by sticking out her tongue at him. Dieter snorted with laughter and did the same.

"Hey," Lisa said, trying to defuse the situation. Peter's face was white, and she could see that he was about to explode. "Come on, kids. Let's just watch the horses, okay? They'll be coming into the ring any second now."

Dieter ignored her. He was glaring at Peter. "Anyway, you can't tell me what to do," he said.

"Me either," Hanni added, crossing her little arms over her chest.

"Oh yeah?" Peter said. "Well, we'll just see about that. No dessert for either of you tonight. Got that? And if you keep acting this way, you won't get any pumpkin pie tomorrow at Thanksgiving dinner, either."

Hanni looked worried about that, but Dieter just scowled. "Maybe you can become Mama's husband overnight," he said sullenly. "But that doesn't mean you can become our daddy overnight, too."

"Yeah," Hanni piped up. "We don't want a new daddy."

Lisa gulped. That sort of comment sounded awfully familiar. She had a vague memory of shouting something at her own parents soon after her father had walked out. Something about how they couldn't expect her to adjust all at once just because he suddenly decided it was time to leave.

*Poor kids,* she thought, for the first time feeling a twinge of pity for Dieter and Hanni. *Life must be totally weird for them right now. Their father left just a year ago, and now Mom has a new husband. No wonder they're taking some of that out on Peter.* Lisa bit her lip, remembering the way her mother's face had sort of crumpled every time Lisa had accused her of driving Mr. Atwood away by complaining too much; the sad look her father got whenever Lisa called him a quitter. *Just the same way I took out my feelings on Mom and Dad when they split up.*

Cringing at the memories, which were surprisingly fresh and raw even after all this time, Lisa leaned toward Greta's children. "Okay, okay," she said soothingly. "I'm sure Peter didn't mean it that way."

"He can't tell us what to do," Dieter repeated stubbornly, turning away from all of them.

Peter shot Lisa a helpless look, but all she could do was shrug. She had no idea how to handle this.

At that moment, they heard Greta calling Peter's name.

Glancing down, Lisa saw her sister-in-law climbing the bleachers toward them, a broad smile on her face. "There you are!" she sang out. "I have been looking high and low!"

"Mama!" Hanni shrieked, jumping up and racing down the bleachers, almost tripping a couple of times in her eagerness. She flung herself into her mother's arms. "Mama!"

Dieter stood, too. "Mama, Peter was yelling at us," he said. "Make him stop."

"Never mind that now, darlings," Greta said breathlessly, hurrying up to Peter with Hanni wrapped in her arms and Dieter clinging to her shirtsleeve. She bent to give Peter a quick kiss. "I have just met a dear old friend from the days when I lived in Oslo," she explained quickly. "She has not seen the children since they were babies. I want to take them to her. You will be here for a moment?"

Peter nodded. "We'll be right here."

"Good." Greta smiled down at the kids. "Come, little ones. We must go see an old friend."

The children went along with her willingly, not sparing Peter or Lisa a backward glance. When they had made their way down the bleacher steps and disappeared into the crowd, Peter let out a loud sigh. "Wow," he said bleakly. "That didn't go too well, did it?"

Lisa smiled at him sympathetically. "It could've been better," she admitted as a cheer went up from the crowd. The first competitor had just entered the ring. "But it's only natural, I guess. It's a tough situation."

They were silent for a few minutes, watching as the rider—a teenage girl on a sharp-looking hunter—completed the simple jump course. Lisa clapped politely along with everyone else as the girl rode out of the ring.

Then she glanced at her brother. He was sitting with downcast eyes, seeming hardly aware of what was going on around him. "You've got to remember, this is really hard for them," she said softly. "They don't understand what's happening, and they have to find someone to blame for their feelings. You should try not to take it too personally."

Peter looked up at her, his forehead slightly creased with confusion. "What do you mean?" he asked heavily. "They hate me. Isn't it obvious?"

"Peter, they're just little kids," Lisa reminded him, reaching over to pat the back of his hand. "They don't hate you. They just resent you right now, and that's perfectly normal. This is all new to them, and they don't know how to handle it."

Another rider was in the ring by now, but neither Peter nor Lisa was watching. Peter stared at

Lisa blankly. "It's new to me, too," he said. "I'm trying, but I just don't think it's working."

"You've got to give it time," Lisa said, thinking back once again to her parents' divorce. "That's really the most important thing. You have to let them get used to the idea that their family has changed, and that it's going to be this way from now on."

Peter blinked. "Wow," he said. "I guess I never thought of it that way before. I've been doing my best to adjust to suddenly having a wife and two kids to deal with. I sort of forgot that they've got to adjust to having me around, too." He looked sheepish. "Pretty immature for an old married guy, huh?"

"Not really." Lisa smiled at her brother.

"How'd you get to be so wise, anyway, little sis?" Peter asked, putting an arm around her shoulders and giving her a squeeze. "Oh, that's right. You've been through this before, right?"

"Yeah," Lisa replied, flashing again to the day her father left.

Peter nodded. "Me too," he said. "But I'm sure it was a lot tougher on you, being right there through the divorce and all. Anyway, you seem to have done a better job than me on that, too. I have to admit, I still haven't gotten past my resentment toward Dad for walking out, let alone worked out what I think about Evelyn."

"Evelyn?" Lisa was startled to hear her brother mention their stepmother. She hadn't been thinking about her at all. "Actually, Evelyn was never a problem for me. I think she's great—I liked her the first time I met her. Besides, she makes Dad happy. I think that's really cool."

Peter gazed at her for a moment, looking slightly skeptical. Finally he shrugged. "Okay," he said. "Now, come on. Let's just sit back and try to enjoy the rest of this horse show."

# ELEVEN

"Well now, Carole," Dr. Durbin said breathlessly as she hoisted one end of a metal park bench. "Is this how you imagined spending Thanksgiving morning?"

"No way," Carole panted in reply, doing her best to keep the other end of the bench from slipping out of her grip. It was heavier than it looked, and she was already wishing she'd thought to wear her riding boots to protect her feet in case she dropped it on her toe. Her thin sneakers certainly weren't going to do much good.

Just as she and Dr. Durbin settled the bench in its assigned spot, a slender young volunteer came running toward them, looking slightly frantic. "Jan! Carole!" the woman called. "If you're finished with that, could you come help us with the lightbulbs for the playground lights? We got the old ones and the new ones mixed up."

"Be right there," Dr. Durbin replied for both of them. After making a few last adjustments to the bench, she hurried after the other volunteer, who was heading for the playground.

Carole followed, still a little breathless from her previous task. It had been that way all morning—every time one job was finished, there seemed to be forty-two others that demanded immediate attention. The group had been working hard all week, but today their efforts seemed to have gone into overdrive. Carole guessed that was because all the volunteers were eager to finish up as early as possible so that they could get home to their families and their turkey dinners.

Carole had been so busy that she'd hardly given a thought to her own Thanksgiving plans. As usual, she and her father had planned to stay home and celebrate quietly, just the two of them. Normally that was the best holiday Carole could imagine. This year, however . . . She shuddered slightly as she imagined yet another gloomy, silent meal with her father, neither of them knowing what to say to the other.

It was a depressing thought, and Carole quickly banished it from her mind as Dr. Durbin passed her a couple of lightbulbs to test in one of the metal lanterns that Hometown Hope's electrician had installed to light the playground's paths and equipment. Carole figured the best way to keep from dwelling on all the problems in her life was just to keep as busy as possible. Fortunately, that wasn't proving hard to do when she was on the job with Hometown Hope.

Just as Carole and the others finished the lightbulb job, Nadine hurried up to them. "Are you guys done here?" she asked. "The rest of the playground is almost ready, too. Lionel and I just need someone to help us hang the swings—we want to make sure they're on straight."

"I'll do it," Carole offered. She turned and followed Nadine over to the brand-new swing set. While most of the playground equipment had needed just a little repair and a fresh coat of paint, the old metal swing set had rusted away to almost nothing by the time they had gotten there. One of the volunteers was a carpenter, and he had designed the old set's replacement—a wooden swing complex that contained a climbing area, a sturdy plastic slide, and half a dozen wooden swings, which were currently stacked beside one of the park's brand-new metal trash cans.

Lionel was already climbing up to the thick top beam of the swing set. When he was ready, Nadine tossed him the ends of the chains and held the swing steady, while Carole watched to make sure the ends were even so that the swing would hang correctly. Working as a team, it didn't take them long to complete the task. Just minutes later, Carole eyed the last swing critically. "Perfect," she declared. "Totally horizontal."

"Great." Lionel smiled and pounded in the final bolt holding the swing in place. Then he slid down the wooden post at the end of the swing set and pulled off his heavy work gloves, brushing his hands on his jeans. "Then I guess that's it," he said. "We're finished."

Carole nodded. "Okay, what's next?"

Nadine laughed. "No, Carole," she said gently. "He's means we're *finished*. The whole park. See?" She waved an arm at the scene around them.

Carole blinked and took a look around. She had been so focused on the swing set that she hadn't even noticed that most of the other workers had wound up their jobs. Aside from a couple of people who were sweeping some newly fallen leaves off the surrounding sidewalks, the entire group was standing around, singly or in small clusters, admiring the results of their efforts.

For the first time, Carole took a good look at what all their hard work had accomplished. When the volunteer group had first arrived on Saturday, the grubby little park had been a total mess. Now it was like a whole new place. Neat gravel paths led in from the sidewalks on each side and wound their way between freshly planted shrubs. Newly laid sod had turned the central area into a lush green lawn. A birdbath and several benches decorated one shady corner, while the bright paint of the playground equipment gleamed in the late-morning sunshine.

*Wow,* Carole thought, running one hand over her dark springy hair. *We really did something here.*

"So, what do you think, Carole?" Nadine asked, coming to stand beside her. "It feels pretty good, doesn't it?' "

"It sure does," Carole replied truthfully. "I can't believe we did all this. It looks amazing! I didn't realize how it was all coming together until right this minute."

Lionel smiled. "I know," he said. "It's that can't see the forest for the trees thing. When you're focused on the details, you tend to miss the big picture."

"But it always sneaks up on you again sooner or later," Nadine said with a laugh. "Surprise!"

Carole chuckled. As her gaze wandered past the playground again, she spotted a small crowd of children watching from the sidewalk. Zani was standing at the front of the group, her dark eyes huge as she stared at the new swing set. "Hey, look," Carole said. "I think the kids want to check out their new park."

"What are you waiting for?" Lionel winked. "Go invite them in."

Carole nodded and started forward. "Zani," she called. "Come here for a second."

Zani looked surprised, but she stepped toward

Carole. "How do you know my name?" she asked shyly.

Carole bent down until her face was level with the little girl's. "Your friends told me," she said. "I remembered it because it's such a pretty name. So, Zani, how would you like to test out the new swing set over there?"

Zani looked awed. "I'd like that."

"Good." Carole smiled, stood, and gestured for her to come forward. "Come on, hop on. I'll give you a push."

Zani quickly complied, choosing the swing on the end near the slide. Carole gave her a gentle push, and soon the little girl was pumping her legs, swinging herself enthusiastically. That was all her friends needed to see. Seconds later, the playground was overrun with chattering, laughing, playing kids.

Carole rejoined Lionel and Nadine, who were watching the children with their arms intertwined. *I wonder if they're thinking about all the kids they wanted to have,* Carole thought, suddenly remembering their story. *I wonder if it makes them sad to see other people's kids playing.*

"This is my favorite part," Nadine said softly, not taking her eyes off the children. "Seeing how much our contribution means to people. It reminds me of all the wonderful things in my life that I usually take for granted."

"That's what we mean about living positively instead of negatively," Lionel agreed, glancing at Carole. "It's times like this that really make you grateful for what you have, and what you can give, if you're just open to it."

"Grateful?" Carole repeated, suddenly remembering what day it was. "Shouldn't that be *thankful*?"

Nadine and Lionel laughed. "You're right," Nadine said. "Happy Thanksgiving, Carole. And congratulations on completing your first project with Hometown Hope."

"Thanks." Carole smiled, feeling better than she'd felt in a couple of weeks.

At that moment her eye caught a flash of movement on the street beyond the playground. Turning to look, she spotted Ben walking slowly toward the park, his hands shoved deep into his pockets.

Seeing him again brought back all her mixed-up feelings in a rush. *I can't believe he's here again,* she thought. *Even though it's a holiday, I was sure he'd spend the whole day at Pine Hollow. . . .*

Suddenly it struck her. For the first time, she really thought about that and what it meant. It didn't just mean that Ben loved being at the stable—that was true enough, and Carole felt the same way. But it also meant that Ben really didn't seem to have a safe, loving, comfortable place to go to when he wasn't at Pine Hollow. Even in the midst of her grounding, Carole couldn't imagine what it might be like not to belong anywhere, not to have that safe place. Her father might be angry with her now, angrier than he'd ever been before, but she didn't doubt for one second that he still loved her more than anyone else on the planet. Nothing could change that.

*But it's more than just me and Dad,* she thought, still gazing at Ben. *There are plenty of other people who care about me and wouldn't let anything bad happen to me—my other relatives, my friends and their families, Max and his family. . . . Ben could have that, too, if he'd just let himself. If he'd just figure out how to be open, to let other people in—to live positively, as Lionel and Nadine would say.*

"Excuse me," she said to the couple, suddenly realizing she'd been guilty of some negative thinking lately herself. "I just want to go say hello to someone."

Taking a deep breath, she walked toward Ben. He didn't see her coming at first—he was busy watching Zani shriek with laughter as a tall, skinny boy pushed her swing higher and higher.

Then he turned his head and spotted her. For a moment, Carole was afraid he was going to walk away. But he stood his ground as she approached.

She stopped in front of him, feeling tongue-tied and shy. Her hands felt as though they'd blown up to the size of Clydesdales—she had no idea where to put them. She shoved them awkwardly into her jeans pockets, mirroring Ben's posture.

"Hi," she said, forcing the word past her dry, nervous throat.

"Hi," Ben returned cautiously. "Uh . . ." His voice trailed off, and he turned his head to glance at Zani, who was still swinging.

Shoving the thought of their kiss to the back of her mind, Carole forced herself to go on. "Um, I just wanted to say Happy Thanksgiving."

Ben looked startled. He cleared his throat. "Er, you too," he replied gruffly.

"Thanks." Carole wasn't sure what to say next. "Um, so how are things at Pine Hollow? How's Starlight?"

"Okay." Ben shrugged. "Rachel. You know. She's doing fine with him."

Carole nodded, feeling a little better despite the terseness of Ben's reply. If Rachel were having any problems with Starlight, Ben would tell her. She was certain of that. "That's good," she said. "How about other stuff? How's Firefly doing with her training?"

Ben shrugged again. "She's coming along."

He didn't mention the fact that Carole was supposed to be helping him train the rambunctious filly, and Carole didn't bring it up, either. Instead, she searched her mind for more questions. Earlier that day she'd been dying for an update on life at the stable. But now, for some reason, she couldn't seem to think of anything more to ask.

Zani saved her the trouble, jumping off the swing and racing over to them. "The swings are great!" she cried, grinning up at Carole.

"That's terrific," Carole replied, smiling despite herself at the little girl's enthusiasm, which had totally overtaken her earlier shyness. "I'm glad you like them."

"Will you push me again?" Zani asked, tilting her head to one side so that a lock of curly hair fell down over one big brown eye. "Really high?"

Carole was about to agree, but she felt a little awkward with Ben still standing there next to her. "I already pushed you, remember?" she said. "Why don't you ask your—er—ah—" She stammered helplessly as she glanced at Ben, suddenly realizing that she still had no idea what their relationship might be. Was he her brother? Her stepbrother? She felt her face turning bright red as several excruciating, endless seconds passed in silence.

"Come on, Zani." Ben's voice was brusque as he reached for the little girl's arm. "We've got to go."

Carole watched helplessly, her face burning, as he led Zani off toward the street without looking back.

———

"Could you toss me the cans of cranberry sauce, Lisa?" Evelyn said. "They're over there on the buffet."

Lisa glanced up from setting the table. "Sure," she said. It was Thanksgiving morning, and the two of them were in the kitchen, which smelled of roasting turkey and baking pies. Stepping around the table, she grabbed a couple of cans off the sideboard and brought them over to the counter, where Evelyn was rinsing out a pretty willow pattern dish. "Nice dish," Lisa commented.

"Thanks." Evelyn looked up with a smile, pushing a strand of damp blond hair off her forehead. "My grandma left it to me when she died. She used to use it for the cranberry sauce every Thanksgiving. We always went to her house in Pasadena when I was a kid—family tradition, you know." She opened the cranberry cans as she spoke, then spooned their contents into the willow bowl and carried it toward the table.

Lisa stood back to let her pass, watching as her stepmother set the bowl carefully and lovingly on the table beside Mr. Atwood's usual place. It was a little strange to hear Evelyn talk about her family's traditions at a time like this. In fact, preparing Thanksgiving dinner with Evelyn was a little strange in more ways than one.

Unbidden, Peter's comments of the day before about resenting Evelyn crept into her mind. But

Lisa quickly banished them. *That's ridiculous,* she thought, turning away to fish some serving spoons out of the silverware drawer. *I don't resent Evelyn or her place in our lives. I like her. She's Dad's wife and Lily's mother, and she's good at being both those things. That's what matters.*

Her thoughts were making her uncomfortable. She almost wished someone else would come in to help them, but that didn't seem too likely. Greta was upstairs, probably on the phone with more of her endless business contacts. Lily was taking a nap in her portable crib in one corner of the kitchen. Mr. Atwood and Peter were settled on the living room couch watching football, which seemed to be distracting them enough to keep them from snapping at each other for a change. In fact, the whole house was downright peaceful. . . .

"Aaaah!" Hanni shrieked, racing into the kitchen with her brother at her heels. "Dieter! Stop it!"

"Tag! You're it!" Dieter shouted, crashing into the table and making the bowl of cranberries teeter as he grabbed at his sister's arm. "Now you have to catch me, or you'll have cooties forever."

Lisa grabbed the cranberry bowl just in time to stop it from falling, quickly pushing it to safety in the middle of the table. She grimaced as she did so—she'd never realized that cooties were an international problem. That thought was almost enough to make her smile—until she glanced over at Evelyn, who looked outraged.

"You two!" Evelyn cried, clapping her hands sharply. "Enough! We're trying to cook Thanksgiving dinner in here, if you don't mind."

"Oh, *Thanksgiving,*" Dieter said in a sarcastic tone, rolling his eyes dramatically. "*Ja,* that is one of their American holidays."

Hanni giggled. "They make them up because they don't like to go to work so much, right?"

"Right," Dieter confirmed with a sidelong glance at Lisa and Evelyn.

The noise had awakened Lily from her nap, and she started to wail. Evelyn, still white-faced and angry, hurried over to pick her up.

Mr. Atwood and Peter poked their heads into the room. "Hey, what's all the commotion about in here?" Mr. Atwood asked, raising his voice slightly to make himself heard over Lily's cries.

Evelyn frowned. "It's nothing," she replied shortly. But as she turned away, Lisa heard her mutter, "This just isn't the way I pictured our first family Thanksgiving."

Lisa gulped, glancing around quickly, but no one else seemed to have heard the comment. *Yikes,* she thought, feeling stranger than ever. She peeked at her stepmother, who was crooning over Lily as she comforted the baby. *I wonder if she was only thinking about Greta and her kids when she said that. Or maybe I wasn't supposed to be here this Thanksgiving, either. Maybe to Evelyn, I'm just another person getting in the way of her perfect family Thanksgiving. Sort of like Greta and her kids are to me here, or like Rafe would be if I were back home.*

She gulped, feeling a knot form in the pit of her stomach. Suddenly she didn't have much of an appetite for turkey and cranberries. And she certainly didn't see a whole lot to be thankful for just at the moment.

*So why are we even bothering, then?* she wondered, glancing around the room. Evelyn was lowering Lily into her crib. Lisa's father and brother were wandering back toward the living room after stealing a few handfuls of pretzels from a jar on the counter. Dieter and Hanni were bickering with each other in German as they left the room. Greta apparently hadn't heard any of what had just happened, because she was still nowhere in sight. Lisa sighed. *Why are we bothering with Thanksgiving dinner at all? Because this is starting to feel like a really pathetic joke.*

# TWELVE

"And Deborah says her editor okayed the by-line," Stevie said excitedly, grabbing her napkin off the table and dropping it across her lap. "Isn't that cool? I'm going to be part of a real byline!"

"Gee, Stevie," Alex said sarcastically as he took his seat at the dining room table. "Do you think you could use the word *byline* a few more times? I think you may be close to breaking a record for using the same word, like, a million times in one day."

Their older brother, Chad, grinned good-naturedly. "Give her a break, man," he said, clapping Alex on the back. "It's not every day our little Stevie gets her name in the paper."

Stevie glared at him but decided to let the "our little Stevie" comment pass. "Whatever," she said breezily. "I know Alex is just jealous because I'm leaving him in my dust once again. Not only am I smarter and better-looking than he is, but now I'm going to be published, too."

Their mother looked up from tossing the salad and laughed. "Okay, Stevie," she said. "Enough with the self-promotion, okay? It is Thanksgiving, after all."

"Yeah," Michael muttered from his seat across from Alex. "And I'll be thankful if Stevie shuts up anytime this decade."

Just then Mr. Lake appeared in the doorway, carrying a large platter holding an even larger roasted turkey. "Okay, gang," he sang out. "The main event is here. Hope everyone's hungry!"

The entire family let out a cheer. "Let's get this show on the road!" Alex exclaimed, grabbing his fork.

"Not so fast, buddy," Mr. Lake said, setting the turkey on the table. "Aren't you forgetting something?"

Michael rolled his eyes and sighed loudly. "Yeah, yeah," he said. "Family tradition. Giving thanks."

Mrs. Lake looked amused. "That's right," she said. "It's time for us all to take a moment to remember all the things we have to be thankful for. Who wants to start?"

"I will," her husband said, settling himself in his seat at one end of the table. He cleared his throat and glanced around the table. "First of all, I'm thankful for my health. And for my job—no matter how much I may complain about the hours. But most of all, I'm grateful for my wonderful, special family—every one of you. My beautiful, talented, intelligent wife; my three terrific sons—yes, even you, Michael, so you can stop rolling your eyes—and of course my soon-to-be-published daughter, Stevie."

Stevie grinned and stood, taking a bow. "Thank you, thank you."

"I'd be thankful if Stevie would sit down and stop bragging," Michael muttered.

Mrs. Lake smiled. "Does that mean you're going next, Michael?"

Michael grimaced, but he sat up a little straighter. "Okay, okay," he said. "Um, I'm thankful that I have my own room so I don't have to listen to Alex tell Lisa how beautiful she is on the phone all the time. And I'm thankful for my new headphones that I got for my birthday. And for getting Ms. Franklin for math this year instead of nasty old Mrs. Karl." He shrugged. "That's about it, I guess."

Stevie smirked. "I'm thankful that Michael will only be thirteen for one year."

"Stevie," Mrs. Lake said warningly. "All right, I'm next. I'm thankful, as always, that we are all here together, happy and healthy. And also for the wonderful adventures, important choices, and learning experiences we've all had throughout this past year, which have brought us to this point in our lives."

Stevie traded a glance with Alex, wondering if their mother was thinking about that party and their grounding. She probably was.

"Me next," Chad said. "I'm grateful that I got all the classes I wanted this semester, and that they changed the requirements so I only have to take two levels of Spanish. Also that my nutty roommate Zeke transferred to Florida State so there's no chance I'll be stuck living with him again." He grinned. "Oh yeah, and I'm thankful for my family—even my crazy fame-seeking sister."

Stevie grinned. Before she could say anything, Alex raised his hand. "All right, don't get her started again!" he exclaimed. "I'll go next. I'm thankful for this family, and for my great friends and my girlfriend, and that I passed my English lit test last week. Also, I'm really thankful that Mom and Dad didn't keep Stevie and me grounded until graduation—even though I totally know we deserved it. Thanks, guys."

Mr. and Mrs. Lake nodded, looking pleased. "All right, Stevie," Mrs. Lake said. "That leaves you."

Stevie shrugged. "Well, of course I second what Alex just said about being grounded," she said. "And I'm thankful for this family. And for Carole and Lisa, the best friends in the world. And for all my other friends, especially Callie and Scott and A. J. And of course for Phil. And for Belle, and all the other horses at Pine Hollow, especially Topside and Starlight. And for Max and Deborah and the kids, and for Red and Denise and the rest of the gang there at the stable, and for being able to ride there. Oh yeah, and also for good old Bear." She paused long enough to pet with her foot the family's golden retriever, who was napping under the table.

Meanwhile, Alex began making soft *tick tick tick* noises under his breath. Stevie ignored him.

"And while I'm at it," she went on, "I should probably say a word of thanks that I got Mr. Knight for homeroom. And that I'm finally starting to get the hang of trigonometry. . . ."

"Is this going to be wrapping up anytime soon?" Michael broke in. "I'm starving."

"Just a minute," Stevie told him. "Let's see, I should also remember to be thankful for my trip to California last summer to visit Lisa. And for rainbows. And of course for fluffy little kittens—"

"All right, Stevie," Mr. Lake interrupted. "Let's wind this up before the turkey dries out and crumbles into dust, okay?"

"No problem, I'm almost done." Stevie smiled apologetically at her father. "Just one more thing, okay? I'm especially thankful that I'll be starting my fabulous career as a world-famous journalist tomorrow with my byline in the Washington *Reporter*."

Everyone groaned in unison. Then they dug into the delicious meal. When everyone had a plateful of turkey, potatoes, carrots, green beans, cranberries, and Mr. Lake's secret-recipe chestnut stuffing, the conversation turned back to Stevie's article.

"You know, Stevie, we've all been teasing you about this byline thing," Mr. Lake said. "But seriously, you know we're proud of you."

"Thanks, Dad," Stevie said.

Chad speared a glazed carrot on his fork and shrugged. "Yeah, but we shouldn't be totally surprised that she's discovered journalism," he pointed out. "I mean, think about it. She's got everything it takes to be a reporter."

Stevie blinked at her older brother in surprise. "Really?" she said. "Thanks, Chad."

Chad shrugged. "Hey, it's the simple truth," he said. "I mean, think about it: You're nosy, opinionated . . ."

"A busybody," Alex added helpfully. "Stubborn."

"Persistent," Mrs. Lake put in.

Stevie pretended to be annoyed for a second, but then she gave in and grinned. "Yeah, you're right," she said. "I really do have a perfect personality, don't I?"

"Oh, that reminds me. I forgot to mention one thing I'm thankful for," Alex said through a mouthful of turkey and potatoes.

"What's that, son?" Mr. Lake asked.

Alex grinned. "I'm *really* thankful that you two didn't let Stevie help with the cooking this year."

"Where is everyone?" Evelyn sounded frantic as she stirred a small bowl of applesauce and set it on the table beside a plastic plate of succotash in front of Lily's high chair. The baby let out a squawk and reached for the bowl with her chubby arms, but it was just out of her reach. "If they don't hurry up and get in here, everything will get cold."

Lisa stuck a serving spoon into the bowl of cranberry sauce and glanced toward the kitchen entrance. The hall was empty, but she could hear the television in the living room and Dieter and Hanni arguing with each other somewhere nearby. "I'll go see if I can round them up," she offered.

Taking one last glance at the table, she hurried out of the room. *At least the food looks great,* she thought. *That's something to be thankful for, I guess.*

She returned to the kitchen a few minutes later, dragging Hanni and Dieter by the arm. "Okay, I found two," she told Evelyn breathlessly. "The others will be along soon. Dad and Peter say there's only a minute left on the clock in the football game, which means they should be here in, like, half an hour. And Greta just wants to make one last phone call before it gets too late in Switzerland. Or is it too early?"

She paused, trying to remember whether the European time zones were ahead of the American ones or behind them. But before she could remember, Evelyn let out a frustrated little yell.

"Is it too much to ask that everyone just get to the table on time?" she cried, wiping one sleeve across her forehead, which was beaded with sweat from the heat of the oven. "I can't believe this. It's Thanksgiving!"

Dieter and Hanni, who had just slid into seats at the table, turned to stare at her in surprise. Lisa wasn't sure what to say. Evelyn seemed really upset. *It's no wonder,* Lisa thought, *if she was expecting some kind of traditional, to-Grandmother's-house-we-go kind of family Thanksgiving.*

"I'm sure Dad and Peter will be in any second now," she said helplessly, glancing over at the table just in time to see Dieter sneaking a large piece of avocado out of the salad bowl near his place. She winced, hoping Evelyn hadn't seen. "Um, and you have to remember, Greta doesn't really understand the whole Thanksgiving thing."

At that moment, Lily let out a piercing squall and started rocking back and forth in her high

202

chair, her arms still waving toward the bowl of applesauce. "Oh no." Evelyn looked as though she, too, might start bawling at any moment. "Poor Lily. It's way past your lunchtime, isn't it?" She sighed and glanced at her watch. "I think I'm going to have to go ahead and feed her. So much for our family dinner."

Dieter and Hanni exchanged glances. "Does that mean we can start, too?" Dieter asked.

"Yeah," Hanni put in. "I'm hungry!"

"No!" Evelyn snapped as she hurried toward the baby. She shot the older kids a disgruntled look. "Just sit there until your parents get here."

"He's not our father," Dieter muttered under his breath. But he didn't really sound angry. As Lisa watched, he turned and made a face at his sister. Then, when Evelyn turned away to get Lily's juice bottle out of the refrigerator, his hand shot out and grabbed two more avocado slices out of the salad. He popped one into his mouth and handed the other to Hanni, who ate it with a giggle.

Lisa smiled, then walked over to help Evelyn with the baby. "Here, I'll hold the juice," she offered, knowing that Lily often knocked the bottle off the high chair tray while she was eating.

"Thanks." Evelyn shot her a grateful look. "Thanks a lot, Lisa. I'm glad you're here, at least."

Lisa couldn't help wondering if she really meant

that. Evelyn was so cheerful and upbeat most of the time that it was often hard to tell what she was thinking. And Lisa realized that she usually didn't even bother to wonder about it. "So," she said hesitantly. "Um, I guess this isn't quite the way you planned to spend Thanksgiving this year, huh?"

Evelyn gave her a rueful half smile as she spooned another bite of applesauce into Lily's mouth. "Not quite," she admitted, sitting back as Lily reached for her bottle and Lisa held it for her. "Last year at this time I was hugely pregnant, so your father just grilled turkey burgers and got take-out potatoes from the supermarket." She sighed. "This year, I wanted to make up for that with a nice traditional meal. I've been planning this dinner for a month." She waved one hand at the impressive spread.

Lisa winced as Dieter drew his hand back from the salad bowl just before Evelyn looked toward him. "Well," Lisa said, sitting back as Lily pushed the bottle away and reached again for the applesauce, "at least the food is traditional, right?" She hesitated. "Though I guess it would be a lot nicer for you if all us extra people weren't here."

Evelyn glanced up at her in surprise, almost missing Lily's mouth with the spoon. "What?" she said. "No, Lisa. Don't be silly." She bit her lip and stared at the baby, who had just grabbed a lima bean off her plate and was gazing at it with obvious delight. "Hmmm. Well, actually, now that you mention it, I guess I am a little overwhelmed by all this. I mean, it's always nice to have *you* here, and it means so much to your father to see you. But . . ." Her voice trailed off as she glanced briefly at Hanni and Dieter, who seemed to be arguing in German. "Well, let's just say that when I dreamed of getting married and having a family, I never realized it could be so . . . complicated."

Lisa nodded. "I know what you mean. I never thought my family was perfect or anything, growing up, but it was still a huge shock when . . . you know." She broke off, suddenly feeling awkward talking to her stepmother about her parents' marriage.

But Evelyn looked sympathetic. "It must have been really tough for you," she said as she leaned over to pick up a lima bean that Lily had just thrown on the floor. "Especially when your dad and I met so soon after he moved out here. And then we got married and had Lily not too long after that. . . . Well, all that can't have helped."

"Maybe," Lisa admitted, realizing for the first time that it was true. "I mean, you've always been so nice to me. I definitely didn't want to, you know, blame you or anything. Especially since my dad didn't even know you when he left Mom. But—"

She broke off again, not exactly sure what she was trying to say. It was weird to think that all this time, she'd been avoiding this exact conversation. Trying to pretend that everything was fine and dandy because it seemed easier than dealing with what she was really feeling. But maybe it was harder to keep it all inside and never deal with it at all.

Before she could figure it out, she heard heavy footsteps hurrying toward the kitchen. A moment later Peter and Mr. Atwood burst in, their faces flushed. "Yee-ha!" Peter cried. "Our guys won!" He traded a high five with his father before taking a seat at the table.

"Mmm," Mr. Atwood said as he took his place. "Everything looks fantastic, honey."

Evelyn smiled, quickly wiping a spot of apple-sauce off Lily's face before straightening up. "Thanks."

"Sorry I am late," Greta said, striding in at that moment. "Please, I hope you were not waiting for me."

"Don't worry," Evelyn said graciously. "Peter and Richard just got here. Have a seat, Greta."

When they were all seated, Mr. Atwood cleared his throat. "Before we start, I think we ought to say a few words of thanks." He smiled at Greta and her kids. "I don't know how much you know about Thanksgiving, but it's traditional to take a moment before the meal to remember some of the things we take for granted in everyday life—family, friends, our health." He turned and surveyed the people seated around the table, his gaze resting on Lisa, then moving on to Peter, Lily, and Evelyn. "And I guess I'm especially lucky this year, because all the most important parts of my life are sitting right here at this table."

Lisa was impressed by the speech. Her father usually wasn't very good at expressing his feelings.

"May I say something, too?" Peter said. At his father's nod, he reached over and took Greta's hand in his. "I just want to say thank you to Dad and Evelyn for welcoming us into your house for Thanksgiving. And I also want to say that I will be forever thankful that Greta and I found each other."

"Thank you, darling." Greta squeezed his hand, then glanced at Mr. Atwood and Evelyn. "I, too, wish to give my thanks to you for making room in your home for my family. In my family, we would say, *Ich will das Tischgebet sprechen,* which means 'I wish to give thanks.' And so I wish to do, for my health, my children, my wonderful husband, and all of you here."

Lisa was even more surprised by Greta's gracious speech than she had been by her father's. Everyone else seemed to be, too. There was a moment of silence as everyone at the table sat in thought.

"Hey." Dieter spoke up suddenly, breaking the spell. "Are we going to eat or what?"

The adults laughed. "Sure," Evelyn said. "Let's dig in. Dieter, would you pass the salad around?"

Dieter grabbed the salad bowl and shoved it toward Mr. Atwood, who accepted the bowl but frowned slightly when he looked into it. "Honey," he said, "was the market out of avocados again?"

Lisa bent her head over her plate to hide a smile as Dieter and Hanni started to giggle wildly.

"Could you please pass the potatoes, Carole?"

Carole looked up from her plate with a start. It had been silent in the dining room for so long, she'd almost forgotten that her father was there. For once, though, her mind was only partly occupied with thoughts of Pine Hollow, Starlight, and the rest. She couldn't seem to stop thinking about the look on Zani's face when she'd hopped onto that new swing for the first time. Or the expression in Ben's eyes when he'd spotted her approaching. . . .

"Um, sure, Dad." Carole picked up the warm casserole beside her plate and handed it over.

Her father accepted it with a nod. "Thanks."

Carole bit her lip. Her father had done all the cooking this year, since Carole had returned home from her Hometown Hope project only half an hour before dinner. As usual, he'd whipped up many of the traditional southern favorites his mother and grandmother had taught him during his Georgia boyhood, and the whole house smelled delicious. But Carole didn't have much of an appetite. Usually holiday dinners were a special time for the two of them, a time to renew their bond and remember Carole's mother, who had died of cancer years earlier. What would they have to talk about this year? Carole had almost dreaded finding out.

Now, though, it seemed they might not talk at all. After covering the weather and food, they had drifted into a silence that had stretched out over ten or fifteen minutes. Colonel Hanson didn't seem to have anything to say, and Carole was almost afraid to try to get him talking. It was a strange, uncomfortable feeling. Would things ever go back to normal between them?

*I wish Dad would get over it already,* she thought with a flash of irritation, poking at the greens on her plate. *Can't he just accept that people make mistakes, and move on?*

Risking a quick glance across the table, she saw that her father's forehead was creased and his downcast eyes looked weary as he shoveled food into his mouth. Carole felt a flash of surprise. When had he started looking so old and tired?

"Dad," she said involuntarily, not even knowing what she wanted to say to him.

He glanced up from his plate. "Yes?" he said. "What is it, Carole?"

She gulped. "Uh, nothing. I was just going to tell you about the park we fixed up," she said, latching on to the first safe topic that came to mind. "Um, the project went really well."

"That's good. Tell me about it," Colonel Hanson said, looking interested.

"Well, it was in pretty bad shape when we got there. I wasn't sure how they expected us to get it fixed up in less than a week." Carole shrugged and fiddled with her fork. "But somehow we got it done."

Colonel Hanson nodded. "That's what's known as teamwork," he said solemnly. "Hometown Hope is good at that. They're a fine group. I'm glad you're working with them."

"I'm glad, too," Carole said, realizing as she said it that it was true. At first she'd thought of the volunteer group as merely a way to get out of the house and distract herself from her problems. But looking back, she realized that she'd actually started to enjoy the work a little over the past few days. It felt pretty good to help other people, like Zani and her friends. Besides that, some of her fellow volunteers were really nice—Lionel and Nadine, Craig . . . even Dr. Durbin had started to feel like a new friend, especially now that Carole rarely spoke to her other friends because of her grounding. "Um, I've met some interesting people. Like this cute little girl, Zani—she lives in the neighborhood, and the park is her only place to play, I think." Ben popped into her head again, but Carole suppressed the thought. This wasn't the time to try to figure out what was going on with him. "And then there's this really nice couple, Lionel and Nadine. They can't have kids of their own, but instead of sitting around and being depressed about that, they decided to start doing this volunteer work instead. Pretty cool, huh?"

"Very cool," Colonel Hanson agreed. He set down his fork and put his hands on the table in front of him, gazing at Carole seriously. "Sort of makes you think about what's really important, hmm? I mean, it is Thanksgiving. . . ."

That was when it hit her. *You know, he's right,* she thought. *Lionel and Nadine know what's important. And I thought I did, too—but maybe I didn't quite get it until right now.*

"Dad," she said abruptly, dropping her fork with a clatter. "I want to say something."

"Yes?" Colonel Hanson was still watching her.

His direct gaze was a little unsettling, but Carole couldn't stop. "It's about—about how I cheated on that test. I know I've said before that I'm sorry, and that's still true." She took a deep breath. "But I'm not sure I ever really admitted that it was all my fault. No matter what I thought might happen

211

if I failed—what you would say, or Max—it was still my choice to cheat, and it was a bad one."

Colonel Hanson looked surprised but pleased. "Well, well," he said, leaning forward in his chair. "I'm happy to hear you say that. To be honest, I wasn't quite sure you got that."

"I didn't for a while," Carole admitted, picking up her fork again and stirring the black-eyed peas on her plate. "I guess maybe working on this volunteer project helped me figure it out. Lionel and Nadine are always talking about living positively, which sounds sort of simple and obvious, you know? But they really mean it. They made a specific choice to be positive, and that helps them make every other choice . . . or something like that. Wait, is this making any sense at all? Because I think I'm starting to confuse myself. . . ."

When she looked up, her father was smiling at her, his eyes shining in a way she hadn't seen in a while. "It makes perfect sense," he assured her. "Carole, you know I could never stop loving you. You do know that, don't you?" He paused for Carole's nod before continuing. "But for a while there, when I found out what you'd done—and that you'd kept it from me—I did start *liking* you a little less than usual."

Carole bowed her head, shame sweeping over her as she thought back to that one small moment that had led to so many horrible hours. "I know," she whispered. "I've liked me a little less lately, too, I guess."

"Well, I'm just glad you've grown up enough to realize now that every action has consequences," Colonel Hanson said. "That's an important thing to learn. And if it took this to teach you, then maybe it will all turn out to have been for the best in the long run."

Carole grimaced. "I don't know about that," she said. "I still wish I hadn't cheated."

"You can't change the past." Colonel Hanson picked up his roll and took a bite, chewing thoughtfully before continuing. "But you certainly can learn from it if you give yourself a chance. That's called getting older and wiser."

Carole nodded, feeling a little shy. Her father's words had made her realize that they were talking to each other in a new way—more like two adults having a mature discussion than a parent talking to a child. That made her feel a little sad—why did everything always have to change?—but proud and nervous at the same time. She was seventeen years old now, almost halfway through her junior year of high school. It was scary to think about how fast time was passing. Before she knew it, she would be graduating. And then what?

*Chill,* she told herself, spearing a few black-eyed peas and popping them into her mouth. *You still have plenty of time to worry about the rest of your life. Right now, you have to get through the next month of being grounded.*

That thought brought her back to earth. She still hated the idea of being banned from the stable until New Year's. But she would just have to deal with it somehow. After all, it was her own fault things had turned out this way.

For the rest of the meal, she and her father chatted about various topics—school, Hometown Hope, her father's latest speech, their relatives. Carole didn't really care what they talked about. She was just glad they were back on speaking terms.

As they were carrying the dirty dishes to the sink, the phone rang. Colonel Hanson answered. "Hello?" he said. He paused for a second to listen to the response on the other end. "Oh," he said. "It's you. Happy Thanksgiving."

There was another pause, and then Colonel Hanson burst out laughing. Carole raised one eyebrow. "Dad?" she said. "Who is it?"

He waved a hand distractedly to silence her. "Oh yeah?" he said into the phone. "Well, I've got one for you: Why did the turkey cross the road?" He paused for a second, grinning and winking at Carole before giving the answer: "Because he was following the chicken!"

Carole groaned. There was no question who was on the other end of the line. Her father had been trading lame riddles and horrendously bad puns with Stevie as long as Carole could remember. But why was Stevie calling now? She knew very well that Carole was grounded and couldn't talk on the phone.

"So what can I do for you, Stevie?" Colonel Hanson said, switching the phone to his other ear as he reached to turn on the sink and refill his water glass. "You know I can't let you talk to Carole." He paused again, for much longer this time, listening. "Oh, I see." He glanced at Carole.

Carole was bursting with curiosity. What was going on?

"Well," her father said slowly into the phone. "I wouldn't normally do this. But I suppose since this is important news . . . and it is a holiday. . . . Hold on a sec, okay?" He lowered the receiver and punched a button on the phone before hanging up the receiver. "Stevie? Are you still there?"

"I'm here." Stevie's voice poured into the kitchen out of the small speaker at the base of the phone, sounding a bit crackly and distant.

"You're on speakerphone," Colonel Hanson said. "Say hi to Carole—she's right here with me."

"Hey, girlfriend!" Stevie called cheerfully. "Happy Turkey Day."

"Same to you," Carole replied, taking a few steps closer to the phone so that Stevie would be sure to hear her. "How's it going?" She still couldn't imagine why her father was bending the no-phone-calls rule. He was leaning back against the counter, calmly drinking his water.

"Great!" Stevie exclaimed. "Guess what? I have big news. Remember I told you how Deborah invited me to go on that interview with her the other day?"

"Sure." Carole shot a guilty look at her father, wondering if he would be mad if he realized Stevie had come to visit her while she was volunteering. But he didn't seem to have caught the meaning of Stevie's remark, so Carole returned her attention to the phone. "How was it? Did you go?"

"Uh-huh. And I ended up cracking the whole case!"

Carole frowned in confusion. She'd been pretty wrapped up in her own problems the other day when Stevie had told her about the interview. "What do you mean?" she asked. "What case? I thought it was about retired show horses."

"It was. But we found out the lady running the farm was ripping people off left and right—mostly by not taking proper care of their horses. So we busted her!" Stevie sounded very pleased with herself. "And since I was the one who figured out what was going on, sort of, and I also helped out with the writing a little, Deborah arranged it so that I got my name in the byline! Isn't that cool? It's going to be in tomorrow's *Reporter*!"

"Wow!" Carole was amazed. Once again, Stevie had managed to find adventure and intrigue simply by going about her daily life. "That's amazing. But what happened to the horses?"

"Don't worry. They're going to be fine now that everyone knows what's going on." Stevie laughed. "I should've known you'd ask about the horses even before you congratulated me on my fabulous new journalism career."

Carole chuckled. "Congratulations," she said. "But I don't know if you can really call one article a career, Stevie."

"Oh, but that's the other part," Stevie put in quickly. "I got such a rush out of this whole thing that I made a decision. As soon as school starts again next week, I'm going to join the school paper! I'm going to be an investigative reporter for real!"

Carole was a little surprised at the news. Stevie could be impulsive, but once she made up her mind to do something, she usually did it. And she had a lot on her plate already—her schoolwork, Belle, Phil, student government. . . . Sometimes Carole wondered where her friend got the energy to keep up with her own life.

Still, knowing Stevie, she would make it work somehow. "That's great, Stevie," Carole said sincerely. "Sounds like fun."

"Thanks," Stevie replied. "Hey, is your dad still there?"

"I'm right here," Colonel Hanson said. "In fact, I was about to spoil the fun by saying it's time to wind up this call, so—"

"Just a second," Stevie interrupted. "I just remembered one more. Why are a turkey's legs so long?"

Colonel Hanson chuckled. "Come on, Lake, you're getting rusty," he chided. "So they'll reach the ground. Of course."

As her father and Stevie burst out laughing at the stupid joke, Carole rolled her eyes and smiled. It seemed that some things never changed. And Carole, for one, was very glad about that.

# THIRTEEN

"Whew! I'm stuffed." Mr. Atwood leaned back and patted his belly. "I don't think I can manage that second piece of pie after all, Evelyn."

"Second?" Evelyn cocked an eyebrow at her husband. "Don't you mean fourth?"

Peter laughed and pushed back his chair. "I'm full, too," he announced. "Everything was great, Evelyn. But now I think I'm going to go collapse on the couch and digest. Coming, Dad?"

"Right behind you." Mr. Atwood climbed to his feet. "What time is it, anyway? I wanted to catch the game between . . ."

His voice drifted off as he and Peter wandered out of the room. Lisa smiled as she watched them go. It seemed that their common interest in sports, along with the surprisingly pleasant meal, had brought them to some kind of real peace with each other at last.

Turning back to survey the table, she groaned.

"Wow. What a mess! No wonder the guys were so quick to make their escape."

Evelyn laughed. "Come on," she said, standing. "If the two of us work together, it shouldn't take long to dump everything into the dishwasher. Then we can collapse and digest, too."

"I will help," Greta announced.

Lisa blinked. She'd almost forgotten that her sister-in-law was still in the room. Dieter and Hanni had rushed off a few minutes earlier, taking Lily with them. They'd said they wanted to help her build a castle in the sandbox out back, and Evelyn had agreed, looking only slightly anxious.

Evelyn smiled uncertainly at Greta. "Thanks," she said. "That would be great. Um, how about if you and Lisa bring the dishes over and stack them on the counter, and I'll rinse them and put them in the dishwasher."

Lisa nodded and stood up, grabbing her own plate and several others. She was halfway to the counter when Greta stopped short in front of her.

"Wait a minute," Greta said. "What are we doing?"

"Um . . ." Evelyn glanced at Lisa for help. "Cleaning up?"

Greta dropped her stack of dishes on the counter and put her hands on her hips, gazing at Lisa and Evelyn. "Yes," she said. "But why?"

"Oh, it's okay," Evelyn said quickly. "Lisa and I

can handle it if you need to go make more calls or—"

"*Nein,* that's not what I mean." Greta smiled. "I mean, why are we doing it, when those lazy men are just sitting on their *Hinterbacken,* burping in front of the television? And after Evelyn spent all day cooking." She clenched one fist and held it over her head. "I say we teach them a lesson—and make them clean up!"

Lisa laughed out loud at the determined expression on Greta's face. "All right!" she whooped, pumping her own fist in the air. "I'm with you. Let's go drag those lazy bums in here right now!"

Evelyn didn't seem to know whether to take them seriously or not. "Oh, no, don't bother them," she said. "We can handle it."

"Nonsense!" Greta said firmly. "Come." Without waiting for an answer, she marched out of the kitchen with Lisa on her heels. Evelyn trailed behind them, still murmuring that she could take care of it.

Peter glanced up as the three of them entered the living room. "Hey, ladies," he said. "All finished in the kitchen?"

"Yes, we are," Greta replied. "Now it is your turn."

Mr. Atwood scratched his head, pretending deep confusion. "Ugh," he grunted in his best caveman voice. "Clean up dinner? Me say that woman's work!"

"Ugh!" Peter grunted in agreement. He pounded his fists on his chest. "Women wash dishes. Men watch football!"

"Oh yeah?" Without warning, Greta leaped at him and started tickling him. Lisa and Evelyn exchanged glances—and grins. Within seconds, they were attacking Mr. Atwood.

Soon they were all laughing so hard that nobody felt like cleaning up, though Mr. Atwood and Peter swore solemnly that they would take care of it during halftime. They all sat together, watching the game and recovering from the heavy meal.

Lisa found her gaze wandering frequently to Greta, who was sitting on the couch beside Peter with her feet tucked up under her. For the first time, Lisa had caught a glimpse of just what it was that Peter might find so appealing in his new wife. *I guess I really haven't been totally fair,* Lisa thought lazily, stretching out on the love seat as she shifted to a more comfortable position. *I mean, Greta is new to us. But we're new to her, too—plus, she's in a whole new country. It's up to me to make her feel welcome. Especially now that I've seen that she does have an interesting, fun, likable side.* She smiled as she remembered Greta leading the charge into the living room. *If only we could find that kind of connection more often.*

Suddenly she sat up straight. Of course! There was one thing that connected her and Greta, whether Greta really realized it or not. "Hey Greta," she blurted out. "I just had a great idea. Want to go riding with me tomorrow? Just for fun—not work."

Greta looked startled. "Riding?" she repeated. "But where?"

"Um, there's a stable not too far from here that rents out some pretty nice horses. I used to go there a lot with friends when I was staying out here last summer." Lisa was already feeling a little nervous about her idea. What was she thinking? Even if Greta agreed instead of turning her down bluntly, what would the two of them find to say to each other during a long trail ride through the woods? Worse yet, what if Greta insisted on bringing her kids along, turning the whole thing into a huge production?

Greta looked as uncertain as Lisa felt. But after a quick glance at Peter, she nodded. "All right," she said. "That sounds . . . pleasant." She leaned over and poked Peter in the side. "Why don't you come, too, *Liebling*? You could exercise off a few of the pounds you ate for dinner today."

Peter pretended to be insulted. "What do you mean? I'm in peak condition. Besides, I already had a full exercise program worked out for tomor-

223

row. It consists of sitting here on this couch and watching other people exercise."

Greta laughed. "Very funny. Now, are you coming? I want to show your sister what a terrible rider you are."

Peter grinned. "Well, if you put it that way, how can I resist?" he joked. "I'm in. But you two have to promise not to tease me too much about keeping my heels up and my earlobes down, or whatever it is you riders are always saying to each other."

Lisa giggled, feeling relieved that Peter would be coming along. *I guess maybe Greta isn't quite ready for the two of us to go it alone just yet, either,* she thought. *But that's okay. One step at a time. . . .*

"I was planning to be home most of the day tomorrow, anyway," Evelyn said, glancing from Greta to Peter and back again. "I could keep an eye on Dieter and Hanni for you if you like."

"Thank you." Greta nodded and smiled. "We would appreciate that very much."

Evelyn looked pleased, and Lisa felt a sudden rush of affection for her stepmother. She was trying really hard at making her weird, unexpected, mixed-up family work, and Lisa had to give her credit for that.

As they were making more detailed plans to go to the stable the next morning, the phone rang. Mr. Atwood was the closest, so he picked up.

"Hello," he said. "Atwood residence." He listened, then smiled. "Oh, hello," he said. "Just one moment. She's right here." He nodded to Lisa. "It's for you."

"Who is it? Is it Alex?" Lisa glanced at her watch, trying to calculate whether the Lakes would have finished their Thanksgiving dinner yet. She put the phone to her ear. "Hello?"

"Hi, Lisa. Surprise! Guess who!" a familiar voice said.

"Skye!" Lisa gasped. "Is that you? Where are you?"

"That's the surprise," Skye replied. "I'm right here in L.A., just like you. My promo tour schedule got changed, and my director wanted me to fly back here so that I can rerecord some dialogue tomorrow morning. So it looks like I have a whole two or three hours off tomorrow afternoon. What about you? Do you have time to get together for a cup of coffee or something, say around two? I know it's short notice, but—"

"That's okay," Lisa interrupted. "That sounds great. I'd love to!"

They quickly arranged a place to meet. As she said good-bye and hung up, Lisa felt a twinge of anxiety. She'd thought that Skye would be out of town through her whole visit. When Alex found out she was seeing him, even briefly for coffee, he would freak out.

*Still, that's his problem,* Lisa told herself firmly as she settled back on the love seat again. *Skye is my friend, and I want to see him. Alex will just have to deal.*

"You were right, Lisa," Greta said the next morning, surveying the neat, low-slung buildings and well-kept fences of the rental stable. "This seems like a very nice place. With some good-looking horses." She nodded at a few horses grazing in a pasture nearby.

Lisa smiled, feeling good about their excursion. "Let's go right in," she said, glancing at her watch. "I called and told the manager to expect us around now."

As they entered the main building, a stout, bearded man hurried forward to meet them. "Lisa!" he exclaimed. "So lovely to see you again, my dear!"

"Hi, Mr. Burke," Lisa replied with a smile. "It's good to see you, too." She quickly introduced Peter and Greta, mentioning Greta's job.

"Wonderful." Mr. Burke peered at Greta as he shook her hand. "And if Lisa says you're a top-notch rider, that's good enough for me. You can have your pick of our available horses."

"Thank you," Greta replied, glancing at Lisa curiously.

Lisa hid a pleased smile. She was sure that Greta

would respect her riding a lot more as soon as she saw her in the saddle, but it was still nice to hear Mr. Burke sing her praises. "I should warn you, though," she told the stable manager, "my brother isn't quite in the same league as his wife."

"I'm not in any league at all, actually," Peter put in, looking slightly nervous. "Um, if you have a nice bicycle I could ride . . ."

Mr. Burke laughed. "I have just the thing," he promised. "Come. Let's get you saddled up."

A short while later, the three of them were mounted and riding out of the courtyard toward a trail through the low, scrubby foothills surrounding the stable. Lisa was riding one of her favorite mounts from the summer, a spirited bay named Fred. Greta was on a strong, feisty quarter horse mare. And Peter was snug in the saddle of a steady old Appaloosa. Despite the fact that his mount seemed unlikely to break out of a slow walk unless a UFO landed on the trail in front of him, Peter looked slightly apprehensive as he did his best to steer his mount along between the others.

"Are you okay there, bro?" Lisa asked.

"Fine," Peter replied distractedly. "Just fine. No problems here."

Lisa grinned. "Okay, if you say so. You just look a little nervous, that's all."

"I'm not nervous," Peter insisted, tightening his grip on the reins as the Appaloosa took a step to the side to avoid a large rock. "This is a piece of cake, really."

"Uh-huh. I think we are lucky he's sitting the right way round in the saddle," Greta joked with an amused glance at Lisa.

Peter pretended to be insulted, but Lisa laughed. "Yeah, I know," she said. "I didn't think he knew which end of a horse was which, either." She shook her head with mock concern. "I don't know, Greta. I think you have your work cut out for you if you plan to turn him into a rider."

Greta chuckled. "Oh, I know," she said. "But I am determined. I think it will only take me the next forty years or so."

Lisa laughed at the joke, but Greta's words struck her in a weird way. They were the words of someone who was in a relationship for the long haul. The very long haul. Somehow, Lisa still hadn't quite accepted the fact that Greta and Peter had promised to be together forever. Forever was a long time.

She glanced over at Greta, who was instructing Peter on keeping his heels down and his elbows in. *Wow,* she thought. *When you think about it that way, I guess maybe it's worth taking a little extra time to get to know her.*

# FOURTEEN

Carole tapped her pencil on the coffee table, reading through the algebra problem one more time. She frowned, trying to remember what her teacher had taught them the previous Friday when he'd given them the assignment. After Carole's busy week of volunteering, school seemed very far away somehow. Almost as far away as Pine Hollow . . .

"Doing okay there, Carole?" her father asked, glancing up from his newspaper. He was seated across the room in his favorite recliner, having a cup of coffee as he read. "Need any help?"

"No, that's okay. I can get it." Carole forced herself to keep her voice light.

*No big deal,* she told herself. *It's not as if Dad never offered to help with my homework before.*

She sighed and scratched her shoulder with the end of her pencil, glancing over at her father quickly. He had returned to his reading and didn't notice her looking.

*No,* she added. *But before the past couple of weeks, I never got the feeling that he was doing it to check up on me.*

It wasn't a happy thought, but Carole knew there was nothing she could do to change her father's wariness except try to earn back his trust. She'd made a start the day before at Thanksgiving dinner, but it was only a start. It would take time—probably a lot of time—and some real effort on her part if she wanted things between them to go all the way back to the way they once were.

*But mainly, I've got to stay positive,* she told herself, her thoughts flashing momentarily to Lionel and Nadine. *After all, despite everything that's happened, I still have an awful lot to be thankful for. I shouldn't forget that. I also shouldn't forget that things are changing, whether I like it or not. I'm growing up, and that means my choices have consequences. They matter more than ever.*

She chewed on her lower lip as she thought about that, her math homework forgotten for the moment. It wasn't as though she was the only one who had to deal with the consequences of his or her decisions. Everyone she knew had to make choices all the time. Sometimes they made the wrong one—like when Stevie and Alex had decided to drink at that party. Other times it wasn't totally clear whether the choice was the right one or not, like Lisa's decision to go to NVU.

Thinking about her friends reminded her about Stevie's big announcement the day before. *I still can't believe she's going to join her school paper,* she thought with a smile. *No, on second thought, I do believe it. Actually, it's a natural. Stevie has the perfect balance of inquiring mind and persistence to track down the big stories.*

She wondered if Stevie might follow in Deborah's footsteps for real someday by pursuing a career in journalism. It was an interesting thought, though it also made Carole feel a little sad. After all, it wasn't so many years before that she had thought all three of them—herself, Stevie, Lisa—might someday choose careers with horses. In her daydreams, Carole had always imagined that Stevie would end up going to law school like her parents and then become an animal rights champion or something. And in those same daydreams, she'd thought that Lisa might make a terrific equine vet. After all, she was good at all her subjects in school, and she was so precise and detail oriented. . . .

Carole sighed, playing with one corner of her math paper. Daydreams were one thing, but this was real life. And no matter how much she wanted her friends to do one thing or another, she knew it would be their decision to become journalists or vets or whatever. Just as it was hers to stick with horses.

*You know,* Carole told herself, *now that I'm feeling like such a wise adult—well, sort of—maybe it's time for me to start thinking more about that particular decision, too. After all, I only have a little over a year and a half left of high school. Then I'll have to start narrowing down my career choices.*

She had known for as long as she could remember that she would work with horses someday. For just as long, she had been torn between all kinds of different ways she could do that. She could be a competitive rider or a vet. She could train for other people or run a boarding stable like Pine Hollow. She could breed or do any number of other things. She'd toyed with the big decision in the past but had always backed away, telling herself she had plenty of time. But now time was getting short, and she knew she was going to have to decide before long. Which did she want to do most?

*I have no idea,* she admitted to herself. *But maybe I should spend some of my free time over the next few weeks trying to figure it out.*

Just then the phone rang, startling her out of her thoughts. "I'll get it," she told her father, who nodded absently as he turned a page in his paper. Carole hurried to the phone on the side table by the couch. "Hello?"

"Hi, this is Craig Skippack," a polite voice responded. "Could I please speak with Carole?"

"Hi, Craig," Carole said. "It's me. Carole."

Colonel Hanson looked up and raised an eyebrow. Carole put a hand over the mouthpiece.

"It's someone from Hometown Hope," she whispered.

Her father nodded, looking satisfied. He returned to reading the newspaper as Carole returned her attention to the call.

"So what's up?" she asked Craig.

"I just got word that our next project was approved." Craig sounded excited. "We start next week. The animal shelter wants us to help spruce up their place—new coat of paint, the whole works. What do you say? Are you in?"

Carole hesitated, but only for a second. "I'm in," she said, realizing she wasn't agreeing only because her father and Dr. Durbin expected her to. She was doing it because she wanted to. It couldn't take the place of riding—nothing could do that—but helping people in a hands-on way was a lot more rewarding than she'd ever expected. She smiled as she remembered Zani's face as she pumped her legs back and forth, reaching for the sky. "Just tell me when and where to show up."

It wasn't hard for Lisa to find Skye once she arrived at the café. She knew better than to expect to see him at one of the outdoor tables, since he would have been mobbed the second he sat down. When she pushed her way through the heavy glass doors into the air-conditioned interior, her gaze fell on a table full of overdressed women in their thirties, all of whom were whispering and shooting glances toward a table in one corner. The waitress working the tables at the front of the restaurant also kept looking toward that particular corner, as did several of the other customers.

Lisa smiled wryly as she followed their gaze and saw Skye sitting by himself, his handsome, square-jawed face bent over a newspaper. She hurried toward him. The table he had chosen was off by itself in front of a small side window.

"Hi," she said.

He looked up, his face arranged into the professional smile Lisa had seen him flash dozens of times at the fans who approached him for autographs. But when he recognized her, the smile relaxed into the more open, genuine one Lisa knew much better.

"Lisa!" he exclaimed, standing up and hurrying around the table. Taking both her hands in his, he leaned down and planted a quick kiss on one cheek before leading her to her seat. "It's great to see you. You look as beautiful as ever."

"Thanks." Lisa sat back and looked him over. "You look pretty great yourself." His blond hair was cut a little shorter than it had been the last time she'd seen him, but otherwise he hadn't changed at all. He was still every inch the handsome movie star who made women swoon from Topeka to Taiwan. But he was also still her friend Skye, the nice, friendly guy she'd known since she was a little more than a kid and he was a teen idol just beginning his career as a serious actor.

"Have a seat," Skye said, gesturing to the chair across from his. "So, how've you been? How was your Thanksgiving?"

"It was okay." Lisa's lips were a little dry, and she was grateful when the waitress hurried over and plunked a glass of water in front of her, staring at Skye the whole time. Lisa took a sip of the icy water, trying to banish the memory of a certain moment the summer before—the day just before she'd returned to Virginia—when Skye had admitted that his feelings for her were starting to go beyond friendship.

Neither of them had mentioned that conversation in the few times they'd talked since, and Lisa wasn't planning to bring it up now. She knew that Skye knew she was in love with Alex, and that was that.

*Anyway, don't be an idiot,* she told herself sternly. *He's not thinking about that little chat anymore. Women swoon over him everywhere he goes. Of course he's moved on. So just get over it already! He's your friend—that's what he's always been, and what he'll always be. A good friend.*

"Just okay?" Skye looked concerned. "You look a little weird. Is anything wrong?"

Lisa blushed, hoping he didn't guess the real reason. "Oh, not really," she said quickly. "Um, I mean, my older brother showed up a few days ago and surprised us."

"Your brother?" Skye shook his head. "I almost forgot you had one. He lives overseas somewhere, right? What's his name again?"

"Peter, and yes, he lives in Switzerland." Lisa cleared her throat. "But that's not all." She quickly filled Skye in on Greta, Dieter, and Hanni. "So that was pretty freaky," she went on. "Especially since Greta isn't exactly easy to warm up to."

At that moment the waitress returned to take their order. Lisa had filled up on leftover turkey after returning from her ride a couple of hours earlier, so she just ordered a cup of tea. Skye asked for coffee and a bagel.

When the waitress had departed, Skye turned back to Lisa. "So this new sister-in-law is hard to know," he said. "But she's also a horsewoman?"

"Uh-huh." Lisa smiled. "Go figure. You'd think the two of us would have tons to talk about. And she does have her moments—like this morning, for instance. We went on a ride over at Clearview Farm, and it was really nice. I even found out she's been encouraging Peter to start writing again. I guess he'd kind of gotten away from it, but it was always his dream to be a writer. Greta thinks he should go for it."

Skye nodded. "Sounds like a good thing."

"I know. It makes me like her more." Lisa sighed, toying with her napkin. "But then at other times she's so hard to talk to. It's like she doesn't care that much about making friends. She can be pretty abrasive sometimes. And those kids of hers . . ." She broke off with an embarrassed laugh, giving Skye a sidelong glance. "Sorry. I guess I'm kind of going on and on about this."

"It's all right," Skye assured her. He reached across the table and patted her hand. "This stuff is important. Sometimes you just need to talk it out, right?"

"Right." Lisa smiled at him gratefully. He really was a pretty amazing friend. "So anyway, I guess what I'm trying to figure out is what's best for Peter. I know he's totally crazy about Greta, and that should give me the answer. But my own feelings keep getting in the way."

"Life's complicated that way," Skye commented, sitting back as the waitress returned with their order.

"Tell me about it," Lisa said with feeling, reaching for the sugar dispenser and dumping a couple of packets into her tea. "I've been dealing with all kinds of feelings this week."

"Oh?" Skye looked interested as he sipped cautiously at his hot coffee.

Lisa stirred her tea. "Yeah. Having Greta suddenly appear in our lives kind of got me thinking about the rest of my family, too."

Taking a deep breath, she went on to tell Skye some of what she'd been thinking and feeling about her parents, Evelyn, and herself over the past couple of days. He was sympathetic, and just having him there listening and caring made her feel a little better about all of it. When she finally wound down, they sat in companionable silence for a moment or two, sipping their drinks.

*I'm starting to figure out that life is all about change,* Lisa thought. *But it's nice to know that some things never change, like being able to count on good friends to be there for you and to care, to always have your best interests at heart.*

"Okay," she said, taking a deep breath and vowing to lighten the mood. "Enough about me. What about you? How's that international superstardom thing treating you these days?"

Skye grinned. "Well, now that you ask . . ."

They chatted about his life and career for a few minutes. Then a thin but insistent beeping interrupted them.

"Oops, that's for me." Skye reached into his pants pocket and pulled out a pager. Glancing at the number on the top, he grimaced. "Ugh, that's what I was afraid of," he said. "I'm really sorry, Lisa. They were having some technical trouble in the studio earlier, and they thought I might have to come back in for another redo, and—Well, anyway, I've got to run. I'm sorry."

"Don't worry about it. I understand." Lisa was disappointed, but she did her best to hide it. She knew that Skye's career could be demanding, and she understood that his free time was always in short supply. "We'll finish catching up next time I come to town."

"Okay." Skye stood up with a smile, pocketing the pager again. "Listen, Lisa. It was really terrific to see you."

"Same here," Lisa said sincerely. "And thanks for listening."

"Anytime." Skye put some money down to settle the bill, then walked around the table and put one hand on her shoulder, his blue eyes caring and warm. "See you." He bent down and brushed her lips lightly with his own.

"See you," Lisa replied softly, a little surprised at the gesture.

She watched as he hurried out of the restaurant, ignoring the whispers and stares of the other customers. When he was gone, she sat back to finish

her tea, feeling happier and more optimistic after
her talk with Skye. Maybe things weren't perfect
with her family right now. But that could change.
They could work things out. All they needed was
some time to get used to the new situation—and a
little more honesty about the period of adjustment.

# FIFTEEN

On Sunday afternoon, Stevie was trotting Belle over some cavalletti in the schooling ring when a familiar car pulled into Pine Hollow's driveway. "Lisa!" Stevie exclaimed, even though her friend was still too far away to hear her.

Stevie rode Belle to the gate and slid out of the saddle. Leading the mare out of the ring, she was just in time to meet Lisa walking up from the parking area. "Hey! Stevie!" Lisa exclaimed, rushing forward. "Hi!"

"Welcome back!" Stevie reached out for a hug, then pulled back and looked Lisa up and down. "So where's your tan?"

Lisa grinned. "That's not all there is to do in California, you know," she said. "Anyway, what's new? I just spoke to Alex on the phone and he said you were here. As always."

"Yep, here I am," Stevie agreed. She grinned wickedly. "So does this mean you're actually more eager to see me than Alex? He'll be totally jealous!"

241

Lisa laughed, looking sheepish. "Actually, he's meeting me here in a little while. We thought we'd take a postholiday trail ride." She paused. "Oh, um—do you want to come along?"

Stevie snorted. "Yeah, right," she said. "And watch you two make googly eyes at each other for an hour? No, you kids go ahead and have a nice time. We can catch up when you get back."

She did her best not to let thoughts of Nicole sneak into her mind. *If Alex thinks Lisa needs to know anything about their new friendship, he'll tell her,* she said to herself firmly. *It's none of my business.*

"Okay, we'll definitely hang out later," Lisa promised. "I have a lot of stuff to tell you about— it was some week out in California. Oh! But do you want to hear the very latest from right here in Willow Creek?" Her face twisted into an expression that Stevie couldn't quite identify.

"What is it?" Stevie asked curiously.

Lisa wrinkled her nose. "It's Mom," she said. "When I got home, I found out that she and Rafe are over."

Stevie gasped. "No!"

"Yes," Lisa said grimly. "From what I can figure out—Mom's not too coherent right now, as you can imagine—Rafe got fired because he was always coming in late and stuff. So then I guess he decided it wasn't worth driving all the way down here just to see Mom if he wasn't coming for work anyway." She shrugged and pulled one finger across her throat. "He ended it right after Thanksgiving dinner. Nice timing, huh?"

"Nice guy," Stevie said sarcastically. "Bummer. Your mom must be a wreck."

"Well . . . yeah. Kind of."

Lisa didn't say anything more, and Stevie didn't press it. She knew that Mrs. Atwood wasn't especially stable since the divorce, and that a lot of the fallout from her emotional issues landed on Lisa. All Stevie could do about that was what she always did—stay ready to support her friend in whatever way she needed.

Lisa glanced at her watch. "Hey," she said abruptly. "You know, Alex probably won't be here for like half an hour at least. Want to go for a quick ride before he gets here?"

"Sure!" Stevie glanced over her shoulder at Belle, who was standing patiently at the ends of her reins. "I'm ready. Let's go get you ready."

Leaving Belle tied outside, they raced in and quickly tacked up Eve. Moments later, they were mounted and riding out of the stable yard into the big south pasture.

"So," Stevie said after a moment. "How was your trip?"

Lisa hesitated, wondering how to answer. "Interesting," she said at last. "Very interesting." She told Stevie about Greta, Peter, Evelyn, and all the rest of it.

When she finished, Stevie let out a low whistle. "Wow," she said, steering Belle around an old stump in the field. "Talk about family drama. So how do you feel about all that stuff now?"

Lisa shrugged. "I'm not sure. Okay, I guess." She bit her lip and glanced at her friend. "Oh yeah, there's one more thing. I had coffee with Skye on Friday. He really made me feel better about everything."

"Oh really? That's good." Stevie looked startled, but she didn't comment further.

Lisa was grateful for that. She knew it couldn't be easy for Stevie to be caught in the middle of the relationship between her twin brother and her best friend. Besides, Lisa herself still wasn't sure what to think about seeing Skye again. She'd thought she was totally okay with the idea that they were just going to be friends. So why did she keep thinking about him—and that casual kiss—at odd moments throughout the day? And why had seeing him made her feel so weird and anxious about coming home to Alex?

*It's just because Alex is so ridiculously jealous of Skye,* she told herself. *He's probably going to flip out when I tell him I got together with him, and it's*

244

*making me nervous. That's all. No mystery there, right?*

"Hey!" Stevie exclaimed, breaking into her thoughts. "I almost forgot—you haven't heard my big news yet. I'm going to be a journalist!"

She excitedly launched into a description of her adventures with Deborah that week. Lisa smiled and listened quietly, not bothering to tell her that Alex had already filled her in on the whole story on the phone.

They discussed Stevie's brilliant future in journalism for a few more minutes before Lisa checked her watch again and decided it was time to head in. Alex would be arriving soon.

She and Stevie parted ways at the back door of the stable. As Stevie led Belle inside for a good grooming, Lisa led Eve around to the front of the stable and tied her to a hitching ring. Then she wandered inside, too, looking for Alex.

She found him in the locker room. He was leaning in the doorway, talking to someone. "Hey!" Lisa said when she spotted him. "There you are."

Alex spun around. "Lisa!" he exclaimed.

He glanced over his shoulder, and, taking a step forward to kiss him, Lisa saw that he'd been talking to Nicole Adams. She frowned as the image of Alex and Nicole slow-dancing at his party, after she and Alex had broken up, flashed into her mind.

But she pushed it away just as quickly as it had come. Alex had been drunk at the time. It hadn't meant anything. "Hi, Nicole," she said politely as she pulled away from Alex's kiss.

"Hey, Lisa," Nicole replied. She glanced at Alex. "Well, see you tomorrow in school," she told him casually. Then she slung her backpack over her shoulder and walked past them, disappearing through the stable entrance without a backward glance.

Meanwhile, Alex was gazing down at Lisa as if he couldn't get enough of looking at her. "Wow," he said huskily. "You look great. I can't believe you're finally home."

"Me either." Lisa moved forward again, wrapping her arms around him and settling her head against his shoulder. It felt good to be back in his arms. It was a warm, safe, happy, comfortable feeling, and for a moment she just let herself enjoy it.

*I'll have plenty of time to worry about the hard stuff later,* she thought, her mind jumping from an image of her mother's tear-stained face to the picture of Peter and Greta waving good-bye to her at the airport, and then to Skye. And of course there was still the whole college issue hanging over her head—her father had let her know in no uncertain terms that they weren't finished talking about that, even if they'd gotten distracted from it for a little while. *Right now, I just want to relax and have a nice time with my boyfriend—enjoy my last day of vacation.*

"Okay," she said, pulling out of the hug at last and smiling up at Alex. "Ready for that trail ride now?"

# ABOUT THE AUTHOR

**BONNIE BRYANT** is the author of more than a hundred books about horses, including the Pine Hollow series, The Saddle Club series, The Saddle Club Super Editions, and the Pony Tails series. She has also written novels and movie novelizations under her married name, B. B. Hiller.

Ms. Bryant began writing The Saddle Club in 1986. Although she had done some riding before that, she intensified her studies then and found herself learning right along with her characters Stevie, Carole, and Lisa. She claims that they are all much better riders than she is.

Ms. Bryant was born and raised in New York City. She still lives there, in Greenwich Village, with her two sons.